George McK. Steele

Rudimentary Psychology

for schools and colleges

George McK. Steele

Rudimentary Psychology
for schools and colleges

ISBN/EAN: 9783337390419

Printed in Europe, USA, Canada, Australia, Japan

Cover: Foto ©Andreas Hilbeck / pixelio.de

More available books at **www.hansebooks.com**

RUDIMENTARY PSYCHOLOGY

FOR

SCHOOLS AND COLLEGES

BY

G. M. STEELE, LL.D.,

PRINCIPAL OF WESLEYAN ACADEMY, WILBRAHAM, MASS.

LEACH, SHEWELL, & SANBORN,

BOSTON AND NEW YORK.

PREFACE.

THIS WORK is designed for students in academies, high schools, and collegiate institutions. The writer, during many years' experience as a teacher in a seminary in which Psychology has been one of his principal branches, has found no suitable text-book, though he has sought it diligently, and has examined many volumes. The experience of other instructors, as reported to him, is the same. Whatever faults may exist in this presentation — and it would be strange if there were not some — it is, at least, very nearly what the writer would desire for his own classes.

It is what its title designates it, RUDIMENTARY PSYCHOLOGY. There is very little effort at original discussion or speculation. It is an attempt to present in a clear and easily apprehensible form, with due regard both to scientific requirements and to the consensus of the best and most recent authorities, the main facts of Psychology. The more abstruse parts of the study have been omitted. Unnecessary technical terms, and such as are difficult to understand, have been avoided, and simple language has been used wherever it did not involve too much circumlocution. At the same time there is no affected juvenility of expression.

The writer has drawn freely upon the best authorities, but he has written very little which has not been through the crucible of his own mind. Among the authors made use of, Dr. Hopkins is the most prominent, and his views have been largely, but not wholly, adopted. Dr. Porter, Dr. Hickok, Sir William Hamilton, Reid, Stewart, Fleming, McCosh, and many minor writers have been freely consulted.

In the arrangement of topics the logical method has not been wholly followed, but rather the order in which the different phenomena present themselves to the mind. There are some faculties and powers of the soul upon which others are conditioned, and which, for that reason, might seem to demand prior consideration, but which are more subtle and abstruse, and less easily understood, than the others, and therefore were better deferred for later explanation and elucidation. Concrete illustrations have been used so far as the limits of the work would permit, as the writer has learned by experience that abstract science without such instances is, to young students at least, of little value.

The work is intended for a one-term study, with daily recitations. This will afford ample opportunity for special instruction, and for amplification on particular points.

A knowledge of one's self is of the first importance from the beginning to the end of education; and a knowledge of one's self is essentially a knowledge of the powers and operations of the soul. That even a high school or academic education should conclude without a certain degree of such knowledge, would be a misfortune. At present our schools are seriously lacking in facilities for this study. Whether this attempt to increase these facilities will be successful, is yet to be determined.

The author desires to acknowledge his indebtedness to Miss Louise M. Hodgkins, professor of English literature in Wellesley College, for the examination of manuscript, and to Professor Benjamin Gill, of Wesleyan Academy, for reading the proof-sheets, and to both for valuable suggestions.

GEO. M. STEELE.

WILBRAHAM, MASS.,
January, 1890.

CONTENTS.

DIVISION FIRST.

THE INTELLECT.

PRELIMINARY CHAPTER.

GENERAL FUNCTIONS OF THE INTELLECT : DEFINITIONS.

PART I.

THE PRESENTATIVE FACULTIES.

CHAPTER I.

SENSE-PERCEPTION.

CHAPTER II.

HOW WE BECOME ACQUAINTED WITH THE OUTER WORLD.

CHAPTER III.

ACQUIRED PERCEPTIONS.

CHAPTER IV.

NATURE OF KNOWLEDGE ACQUIRED BY SENSE-PERCEPTION.

CHAPTER V.

ATTENTION.

CHAPTER VI.

THE INNER-SENSE.

CHAPTER VII.

CONSCIOUSNESS.

PART II.

THE REPRESENTATIVE FACULTY.

CHAPTER I.

THE REPRESENTATIVE FACULTY DESCRIBED.

CHAPTER II.

LAWS OF ASSOCIATION

CHAPTER III.

FORMS WHICH THE REPRESENTATIVE PRODUCT ASSUMES.

CHAPTER IV.

RELATION OF THE IMAGINATION TO SOME OTHER FACULTIES.

CHAPTER V.

UTILITY OF THE IMAGINATION.

CHAPTER VI.

CULTIVATION OF THE IMAGINATION.

PART III.

THE ELABORATIVE FACULTY.

CHAPTER I.

THOUGHT AND THINKING.

CHAPTER II.

CONCEPTION AND CONCEPTS.

CHAPTER III.

JUDGMENT.

CHAPTER IV.

REASONING AND INFERENCE.

CHAPTER V.

INDUCTION.

CHAPTER VI.

DEMONSTRATIVE AND PROBABLE REASONING.

PART IV.

THE REGULATIVE FACULTY.

CHAPTER I.

NATURE OF THE REGULATIVE COGNITIONS.

CHAPTER II.

THE FACULTY WHICH FURNISHES THESE COGNITIONS.

CHAPTER III.

PRODUCTS OF THIS FACULTY.

DIVISION SECOND.

THE SENSIBILITIES.

CHAPTER I.

GENERAL CHARACTER OF THE SENSIBILITIES, AND THEIR RELATION TO THE INTELLECT.

CHAPTER II.

THE EMOTIONS.

CHAPTER III.

THE EMOTIONS — CONTINUED.

CHAPTER IV.

THE MORAL EMOTIONS.

CHAPTER V.

THE APPETITES.

CHAPTER VI.

THE DESIRES.

CHAPTER VII.

THE BENEVOLENT AFFECTIONS.

CHAPTER VIII.

THE MALEVOLENT OR MALEFICENT AFFECTIONS.

DIVISION THIRD.

THE WILL.

CHAPTER I.

GENERAL CHARACTERISTICS OF THE WILL.

CHAPTER II.

CHOICE AND MOTIVE.

CHAPTER III.

MAN AS A FREE AGENT.

CHAPTER IV.

THE WILL NOT A SUSCEPTIBILITY, BUT A POWER.

CHAPTER V.

MORAL CHOICE.

CHAPTER VI.

COMPLETE INDIVIDUAL LIBERTY.

CHAPTER VII.

NECESSARY IDEAS PRODUCED BY THE COMBINED ACTION OF THE INTELLECT, SENSIBILITIES, AND WILL.

PSYCHOLOGY.

INTRODUCTORY CHAPTER.

MEANING AND SCOPE OF PSYCHOLOGY.

Psychology is the science of the human soul. The term soul is used here rather than mind, as more obviously covering the whole subject of inquiry. As Dr. Porter says, the terms **Science of Mind, Mental Philosophy,** and **Mental Science** are apt to be applied only to the power of the soul to know — to the intellectual faculties — and are not generally used with reference to the capacity to feel and to will, or for its functions taken together. *Psychology defined.*

As just stated, Psychology is a **science**. It is important to understand definitely what is meant by science. The general meaning, of course, is knowledge. But science as used among scholars is something other than this. It means knowledge systematized and classified, embracing also a knowledge of laws, causes, and relations. While often used as substantially synonymous with **Philosophy**, it yet differs from it in this respect, that Science pertains more to matters of fact, and Philosophy to speculative matters. Perhaps we may be justified in saying that Philosophy deals with truth, Science with facts. Philosophy deals also with first principles; that is, the principles which are prior to all science, and which underlie all *Psychology a science.* *Philosophy as distinguished from science.*

knowledge. It is scarcely possible, then, to pursue the study of any science without an implied philosophy.

The first thing to be done in the study of any science is to observe the **Phenomena**. By phenomena we mean sim-

Phenomena to be studied first.

ply those things which present themselves to our powers of intelligence, — those which appear. We classify these and endeavor to ascertain the causes of them, and the laws and principles by which they are governed. We must pursue this course in the study of the human soul. The peculiarity of this

Observation of psychical phenomena by a faculty of the soul.

study is that our observations of the phenomena of the soul are to be made by one of the faculties of the soul itself. We have a distinct faculty, the function of which is to take cognizance of the operations of the soul. Popularly it is known by the name of **Consciousness**, but scientifically this term has a broader signification, as will be seen when we come to study it more particularly. The faculty is called more definitely by the name of the **Inner-Sense**. By it we gain all the knowledge we have of the phenomena of the mind or soul.

OF THE DIFFERENCE BETWEEN MATTER AND MIND.

Is there any good reason for believing in the existence of **mind** or **soul** as something separate from **matter**? Mate-

Materialistic arguments.

rialistic philosophy answers this question in the negative. It asserts that there is nothing in the universe but matter, and that what we call mind, soul, spirit, is only a form, or perhaps some function, of matter. The main arguments for this doctrine are as follows: 1. The soul is connected with a body. 2. It is developed with the body. 3. It is dependent on the body for its knowledge and enjoyment. 4. It is also dependent on the body for its energy and activity. 5. And finally, that we know nothing about soul, while we have a definite knowledge of matter.

To these arguments it may be replied : That while we admit that the body is a condition for the soul, Counter and that the latter is dependent to a certain arguments. extent on the former, still there are many conclusive reasons for believing it to be a separate existence.

1. While by sense-perception we know nothing about the soul, except its operations, we still know quite as much about it as we know about the body. The only We know as intelligence we have concerning the latter, ex- much about cept the fact of its existence, is the qualities about the and properties which appeal to the several senses. body. The same is true concerning the mind. We know by the Inner-Sense only its energies. The knowledge of the substance in both cases comes to us by the very constitution of the mind itself — we know that such substance or substances exist, as soon as we cognize the qualities. It is in both the same. The Inner-Sense apprehends certain operations constituting mental phenomena, and we at once and necessarily know that these phenomena have a basis, a substance, just as we perceive certain qualities of matter; and there necessarily follows in the mind the knowledge that there is a substance in which they inhere. If either of these be known more If either directly than the other, it is the soul, since the known more Inner-Sense gives us the phenomena of this directly than the other, it directly ; while in the case of matter the Inner- is the soul. Sense must first be cognizant of sensation before perception can apprehend any external phenomena.

2. The two sets of phenomena are radically different in
The two sets of phenomena radically different. many respects; in this, particularly, that those of matter are mainly properties and qualities, while those of soul are energies and activities.

3. The soul distinguishes itself from matter. It is clear to itself that it is not matter. It knows, as certainly
Soul distinguishes itself from matter. as it knows anything, that the perceiving agent is not the same as the material objects which it perceives. It also resists the forces and movements of its own body, and in so doing distinguishes itself from that which it resists.

4. The laws of matter are not compatible with the phenomena of soul. Take the law of inertia, which is an
Laws of matter and those of mind incompatible. essential law of matter. A body will continue in a state of rest or motion, whichever it may be, unless some force outside of itself operate upon it and change that state. The soul is subject to no
The soul self-active. such law. It is self-active. It knows itself as acting voluntarily. It acts from within by an energy of its own, and not merely as it is acted upon.

These are only a few of the reasons for believing that the soul is something entirely different in essence from the body.

One of the principal reasons why we know less about the character of the soul than we know about matter,
Reasons why we seem to know more about matter than mind. notwithstanding the fact that the former lies proximate to the consciousness, while the latter does not, is that the operations of any soul can be observed by only one person, and that one the subject of its operations; while material facts and qualities can be perceived by several at the same time. They can thus make them easily and at once matters of

comparison and discussion, and so become quickly familiar with them. It also tends to greater accuracy, since one's discernment may supplement, and so correct, that of another. We do not dwell much upon subjects concerning which we cannot have a communion of interest with others about us. Especially is this the case early in life, and with persons who have no great mental discipline. We do not naturally give much thought to anything unless our attention is called to it by the action or suggestion of those about us; and when the subject is any act or characteristic of our own minds there is no one to observe it but ourselves, — hence no one to call our attention to it, or to make suggestions concerning it. For these, and possibly other reasons, we become habituated to think and talk about the external very much more than the internal, — the material rather than the spiritual.

RELATION OF THE SOUL TO THE BODY.

1. In man the body is a condition for the soul. It is a principle laid down by Dr. Hopkins, that "those forces, and forms of being, and faculties and products, are lower which are a condition for those which are conditioned upon them." The whole structure of the universe proceeds on this principle, and herein the unity of the *Cosmos* is found. Among the great forces gravitation is a condition for cohesion, gravitation and cohesion for chemical affinity, and all these for vegetable life, and this with those, for animal life, and all for man. This does not imply an identification of the conditioning and the conditioned, nor that the former is the cause of the latter. The foundation is a condition for the house, but it is not the house,

Law of conditioning and conditioned.

Condition not identified with conditioned.

nor the cause of it. Much less is the house identical
with the foundation. It is furthermore evident that the

Conditioned
something
more than
the condi-
tioning.

conditioned is in general something more than
the condition. Cohesion is gravity plus something quite other than gravitation. So of man
as the conditioned of animal; it is animal plus
something else, and this something else is rational soul.
Still, as a house cannot exist without a foundation, and as
cohesion is impossible without gravitation, so, as far as we
can see, the human soul is conditioned on the human body.

2. The various parts of the body are instruments or
means for the operations of the soul. The brain, the nerv-

Members of
the body
instruments
of soul.

ous system, the several senses, and all the
necessary concomitants and conditions of these,
are also conditions and means for the soul's
action. The body is connected with the soul, and thus
brought into this operative relationship by the principle of

Life and
organization.

life. The existence of the soul is not necessarily dependent on this, any more than is the
matter of which the body is composed. But the organization of the body is so apparently dependent on life,
that we nowhere find the latter where the former does
not exist; and on the cessation of life, disorganization
begins.

3. The various powers of the soul are first called into
exercise by the organs of sense. Were there no capa-

Sensation
a condition
for psychical
activity.

bility of receiving impressions from without,
the soul, though possessed of susceptibilities,
would never act, and consequently would be
unconscious of its own existence. But having once been
called into action by these impressions, it is no longer
wholly dependent on them for its activity. The inner-

sense, the discursive faculties, reason and memory, begin to work as soon as there is anything to work on, or any occasion; and this occasion is furnished by the first impressions from without.

DIVISION OF PSYCHICAL PHENOMENA AND POWERS.

There are three forms of psychical manifestation, — the Intellect, the Sensibility, and the Will. These follow the principle of conditioning and conditioned, to which reference has been previously made. We have no feeling, that is, no action of the sensibility, only as we have knowledge, which is a product of the intellect. There can be no interest, no desire, or any delight, in that of which we know nothing. So, also, we make no effort, and put forth no activity, except as we have both knowledge and feeling. We act in view of motives, but motives are of the sensibilities.

Three forms of psychical phenomena.

No feeling without knowledge.

No action without knowledge and feeling.

We are to guard here against the thought that there is a division of the soul into parts, of which one is to be regarded as Intellect, another as Sensibility, and the third as Will. The soul is an indivisible unit. It has no parts; it does not act in sections. Whatever activity or phenomena it has is of the whole. The soul as intellect knows; as sensibility it feels; and as will it chooses, and puts forth volitions. It is the soul, and not any part of it, that does each of these.

Not a partitive division of the soul.

DIVISION FIRST.

THE INTELLECT.

PRELIMINARY CHAPTER.

GENERAL FUNCTIONS OF THE INTELLECT — DEFINITIONS.

It is by the Intellect that we **know**. But what is it to know? It would be impossible to answer this question intelligently, except to a person who already in some sense understands the answer. There is *What is knowledge?* nothing out of a knowing mind to which it can apply. Eminent philosophers have answered the question by saying it is " to be certain of something." This seems to be little more than a synonyme, but it serves to bound off knowledge from some things liable to be mistaken for it which it is not. It is not belief, or opinion, or conjecture. " Knowledge," says Whately, " implies three things, — 1st, Firm belief; 2d, Of what is true; 3d, On sufficient grounds. If any one is in doubt, for example, *Incompatible* respecting one of Euclid's demonstrations, he *with doubt.* cannot be said to *know* the proposition proved by it; if, again, he is fully *convinced* of anything that is not *true*, he is mistaken in supposing himself to know it; *Not synony-* lastly, if two persons are each fully confident, *mous with* one that the moon is inhabited, and the other *conviction.* that it is not (though one of these opinions must be true), neither of them can properly be said to *know* the truth, since he cannot have sufficient *proof* of it."

Knowledge is not the same as **Truth**. This is evident

from the fact that truth is frequently the object of knowledge, the thing to be known, and it would not
Differs from truth. be quite reasonable to assume that the knowledge and the thing known are identical. Truth is the
reality of things, and is the same, whether known or not.
New truths are being constantly found out, but until
found out they are not known. Then again truth is not
knowledge when it is not certitude. As we have seen,
man knows only what he is certain of. There are actual
truths of which he is not yet certain; hence there is no
knowledge respecting them.

" Knowledge supposes three terms: a being who knows,
an object known, and a relation determined be-
Three terms implied in knowledge. tween the knowing being and the known object.
This relation properly constitutes knowledge." [1]

But it is not the whole of the business of the Intellect
to know. The greater part of its operations are subsidiary
Not the sole function of the intellect to know. to knowledge, and many of these operations
stop short of actual knowledge. We may ap-
proximate certainty to a greater or less degree,
and even much of what we take for granted and act upon
as if we knew it, is not knowledge in its strict and scientific sense. We search for knowledge; we investigate,
and reason, and compute; we examine, and compare, and
generalize, and do many other things with the intellect,
the result of which is sometimes knowledge, but more
frequently it is belief, theory, or conviction; and sometimes, perhaps, it is none of these.

There are several **Terms** of frequent use in the
study of psychology, some of which have already ap-
Terms to be defined. peared in the preceding pages, and others
we shall find as we go on, which I take this

[1] Fleming.

opportunity to define and describe. Psychology and Phenomena have been previously explained. Correlative with the latter is **Substance** or substratum. This term is used to denote the unknown basis which underlies all phenomena or properties of which the mind takes cognizance, whether internal or external. We get no knowledge of it by any of the senses, nor by any generalization or judgment or reasoning. The knowledge of it arises spontaneously in the mind whenever there is a cognition, through any means, of any phenomena whatever. The mind itself furnishes this knowledge on the proper occasions, because it is constituted to do so.

Meaning of substance.

As included in phenomena we have cognitions to which we give the names of quality, property, attribute, etc. **Quality** is that in a substance which appeals to the power of apprehension in us, and which distinguishes one individual from another, or one class from others. Qualities may be essential or accidental. By the former we mean those characteristics which a thing cannot lose without ceasing to be, — for instance, body must have extension; man must have rationality. By the latter are meant those aptitudes and manners of existence which substances may have at one time and not at another, or which some other aptitudes might be put in the place of, and yet the object would not cease to be. — as a white house, a sick man, a cloudy sky.

Quality, attribute, property.

Classes of qualities.

Attribute is very nearly a synonyme for quality, only perhaps more likely to be used in speaking of qualities of a higher type and more dignified character, as the attributes of God.

Property has reference usually to some peculiar quality, but is frequently used coextensively with quality in general. As matter of fact, these terms are largely used in popular discourse and conversation as synonymous.

Subject and **Object** are terms frequently occurring in this study, as also their derivatives, **subjective** and **objective** By the former is meant the soul as perceiving, observing, thinking, and by the latter that about which the soul is thus occupied, whether it be external or internal. The object is also the product of the mind in thinking, even when no material object is implied. As, for instance, a man has been studying and investigating the cause of earthquakes. He has finally arrived at what seems to him an explanation of the phenomena. He has formed a theory. This is now objective, while his previous processes have been subjective. Generally, the thinking or knowing entity is the subject; that which it thinks about or knows is the object. So of the terms **subjective** and **objective**, though these as used are somewhat more elusive. There are some words which have both a subjective and an objective meaning; as **Beauty** is used either for the quality in the object which causes the peculiar feeling in the mind, or for the feeling itself. In the former case it is objective beauty, and in the latter subjective beauty.

Subject and object.

But a caution, and perhaps a modification, of what has been said, is necessary here. When the mind is occupied about its own processes, it will be seen at once that the subject and the object are the same. The mind in this as observing and thinking about itself is the subject, while the mind as being observed and thought about is the object. For the most part, philosophers have denominated the mind as thought about, as subject-object, and some, in order to make a symmetrical

The mind sometimes both subject and object.

nomenclature, have called the external object the object-object, though this latter designation seems hardly necessary.

We have another set of words closely related. The first of these is **Power**. It is in general an ability to produce a change. It is not necessarily that which is at any given time producing the changes, but that which renders the subject of it competent to produce changes. As, for instance, I have power to walk, though at present I am sitting still. Power is by a considerable number of writers represented as active and passive; the latter indicating a capability of being changed. But this, it seems to me, is better to be designated as **Susceptibility**, which I would thus define. Power.

Faculty is closely akin to power. All faculties are powers, but, according to Reid, not all powers are faculties. He regards the word *faculty* as properly applied to those powers which are original and natural, and which make a part of the constitution of the human mind. Dr. Hopkins teaches that a faculty is some power of the mind under the control of the Will. Thus he would not call Consciousness a faculty, nor does he so regard that power by which the mind becomes possessed of necessary ideas. In this he does not agree with either Reid or Hamilton. Dr. Wayland applies the term to all the powers and susceptibilities of the mind, going to the other extreme. It will be sufficient for our purpose if we define faculty as *the power of the mind to act*. Faculty.

Capacity has a kindred signification. Literally it means *room for*. It is substantially synonymous with what I have previously called susceptibility, or what Reid calls the passive power of the mind. Meaning of capacity.

The relationship of these three terms may be briefly
stated thus : power is active and passive ; faculty is active power ; capacity is passive power.[1]

The three
terms
compared.

DIVISION OF THE INTELLECTUAL PHENOMENA.

These will be treated in three parts, —

    I. THE PRESENTATIVE FACULTY.

    II. THE REPRESENTATIVE FACULTY.

    III. THE ELABORATIVE FACULTY.

    IV. THE REGULATIVE FACULTY.

[1] Fleming.

PART I.

THE PRESENTATIVE FACULTY.

CHAPTER I.

SENSE-PERCEPTION.

THE **Presentative Faculties** are those powers of the mind by which knowledge comes to us directly from simple observation. They are subdivided into **Sense-Perception**, and what is popularly called **Consciousness**, but more properly the **Inner-Sense**. The former gives us cognitions of the world of matter, the latter of the world of mind.

Presentative faculties described.

One of the great questions of Psychology is, How does the soul come into communication with the outer world? How can immaterial mind come into relations with material substance, so that the former shall receive impressions from the latter? The answers to this question have been various. Like most other subjects pertaining to our constitution and relations, it is involved in more or less of mystery. It is not likely that this mystery, under present human limitations, will ever be absolutely cleared up. But we can at least trace the outlines of the process, and note a considerable proportion of the attendant phenomena.

How can the soul come into communication with the external world?

We observe, first, that there are several bodily organs and instrumentalities concerned in this process. To begin at the outer surface, we find the organs of sight, of hearing, of smelling, of tasting, and of touch. Certain qualities or properties of matter affect these in

The senses.

ways corresponding to the constitution of the several organs. We next observe that these organs are all inti-
The senso-rium. mately connected with what is called the **Senso-rium.** This consists of the brain, spinal column, and a system of nerves running from these to every minute part of the surface of the body, and to most of the internal points. When any outward object or quality makes an impression upon its corresponding sense, it affects one of
Result of sensation. the nerves, which is so nearly like a telegraphic wire that through it an effect is instantly pro-duced in the brain. We cannot trace this series of physical effects any further. We only know that with the vibration of the nerve and the effect on the brain, there comes a change in the mind; we know ourselves to be in a new state. We say we are sensible of it, or conscious of it, and that is all we immediately know.

This is what we call a **Sensation,** and the general name by which we designate this whole class of changes thus pro-
Sensation a state of mind. duced in the mind is **Sensations.** Thus, if a rose is brought near us for the first time, even if we are not able to see it, the odor given off from it somehow affects the olfactory nerve, and produces a peculiar state of mind. We apprehend this change by the Inner-Sense, but this is all that we at first know. We are not, on the supposition we are now making, aware that there is any outward object that causes it. The effect, so far as appears, may have been produced by some internal cause. So if, for the first time, we hear the music of an organ, the only cognition we have is of a state of mind, and we do not know that it comes from without.

It is only after some experience, and the combined action of our senses, that we learn to refer these states of mind, or internal changes, to some object in the external world. Here we have **Perception.** We wish to get a clear distinction between Sensation and Percep- tion, and, as well, the exact relation of the two processes.

Perception.

Sensation *is a state of mind produced by some external ob- ject or influence operating upon the sensorium, and is imme- diately successive to a change in some organ of sense.* **Perception** *is an act or process of the mind immediately successive to a sensation, by which we refer this sensation to something external as its cause.*

Sensation and percep- tion defined.

It is sometimes said that Sensation is subjective, and Perception objective. But this needs qualification. Per- ception, as well as Sensation, is subjective; but the knowledge we get by perception is of exter- nal, outer, or objective things, while Sensation is exclusively subjective, and implies no knowledge of ex- ternality. Dr. Hopkins says that Sensation is a movement from without inward, Perception is a movement from within outward.

Sensation subjective. Perception objective.

CHAPTER II.

HOW WE BECOME ACQUAINTED WITH THE OUTER WORLD.

BEFORE Sensation can be of any use to us in the way of increasing our knowledge, or before Perception can properly avail as a faculty of cognition, we must somehow know that there is an **external world.** How do we acquire this knowledge, is the immediate present question.

By superficial thinkers, and, indeed, by many who are not superficial, it is claimed that we come to this knowl-

Not directly through one or more of the senses.

edge through one or more of the senses, as touch or sight. Dr. Wayland held that sight was immediate perception and not sensation. But I believe his view is sustained by very few good authorities. If, as has been stated, sensations are wholly subjective, and give no knowledge of external things, there must be some other way of accounting for this knowledge. That the sensations do not give this knowledge directly may be made evident by observing the process of sensation through the several organs.

Let us take first the sense of **Smell** as being, perhaps, the simplest. An odorous body, say a rose, is brought

Sense of smell.

near the person. This odor affects the olfactory nerve, as before described. Immediately a sensation is experienced, — a new state of mind. Of this the person affected becomes aware by the Inner-Sense. But this is all that he is aware of. There is in this no intimation of any external cause. So far as the individual is concerned, the new state may be simply the result of an internal change. It is true that when once we have learned that there is an outer world, and have associated the sense of sight with that of smell, then, by observing that whenever the rose is present, the same state of mind occurs, and that it does not occur when this is absent, we come to regard the presence of the rose as the cause of this particular state of mind, and the state of mind, or sensation, becomes the recognized sign that the rose is present. But neither of these is supposed in the present illustration. We are considering the sense of smell by itself, and are not yet presumed to have discovered an external world. Clearly, this sense by itself gives us no such knowledge.

Gives no intimation of externality.

Let us next observe the operation of **Taste**, the sense of **Flavor**. There is some difficulty in studying this, as it can never be wholly separated from the sense of Touch. Any object which we are to taste must, in order to affect the organs of taste, *touch* the mouth and tongue. But we may easily separate, in our minds, the two sensations. In taste, the parts affected are the tongue, the palate, and the pharynx. The mucous membrane of these parts is thickly covered with *papillæ*, and the nerves running from these, as from the organs of sensation, convey the effect to the brain, and hence the sense of taste. Evidently here, but not quite so evidently as in the case of smell, the state of mind is the only thing cognized. It cannot by itself, and before other experiences, give any intimation of a cause in the outer world,

Sense of taste.

for the reason that an outer world is not yet cognized. Nor does this, of itself, intimate the outer world.

The same result will be arrived at in the case of Hearing. Some sonorous body produces vibrations in the air which affect the auricular apparatus. The effect may proceed from a musical instrument. There is a corresponding effect in the mind. But this gives not the slightest intimation of being produced by anything external to the mind. So far as appears from the sensation itself, it is wholly within the mind itself.

Sense of hearing.

Nothing external intimated.

So far, there is little difficulty in accepting the view that the senses themselves give us no knowledge of the outer world. But now we come to the sense of Sight, and shall, perhaps, find the opinion less plausible. Some writers have stoutly insisted that this sense certainly gives us direct cognition of the object seen. The eye, by its very constitution, gives us a larger range of sensations than any of the foregoing senses. Being mobile, it seems to have a larger variety of sensations than the others, and perhaps it does. Still it may not have quite all that it seems to have. By experience and the co-operation of the other senses, we acquire the power to perceive by the eye, not only the color but the form, the size, and many other qualities of a visible object. But the proper quality that appeals to the eye is Color. Dr. Hopkins favors the opinion that the eye properly gives only the sensation of color. "Suppose the eye were set in stone and held fixed. . . . Nobody supposes that the eye originally gives form in more than one dimension, — that we see a globe or cube as such. It could then be but a colored surface.

Sense of sight.

Color is what appeals to the eye.

But under these circumstances, what could then be known of surface or extension? Could the form be anything more than the form of color, and would that be form at all? I think not." If this be so, then color is the only thing that affects the eye in vision, and that effect is a simple sensation, a state of mind which in itself gives no intimation of externality.

In **Touch**, as it appears to some, externality is obvious. But we are to consider that when we touch a thing, there is generally something besides simple tactual *Sense of* effect, such as roughness or smoothness, cold *touch.* or warmth. There is also **Pressure**. It is true we can conceive of simple touch separate from pressure. *Something* In such case we are affected by the tactual *besides tact-* quality and nothing else. If we can regard *ual effect.* this alone as the effect of touch, we shall find that we have here, as in the other senses, only the sensation, a state of the mind which intimates nothing separate from itself.

We have now examined the operations of all the senses, and have, so far, discovered no way in which the mind or soul gets any knowledge of externality. Sen- *The knowl-* sation does not give it, nor, so far as I can see, *nality not* does it come in connection with the operation *through* of any or all of the senses. How, then, does it *but through* come? *resistance.*

Any spontaneous or instinctive movement from within is certain to be met by some *resistance, pressure against, or modification of that movement.* It is then that the individual discovers that he is not the only being extant, — that there is something besides and exterior to himself. He has found an outer world, and he is not long in distinguishing it into

parts and individual objects. This pressure, resistance,
Accompanied by touch, yet separate from it. and modification of his movements is very likely to be accompanied by **Touch**, and is yet separate from it. Still, by touch and sight principally, and by the other senses subordinately, he learns that when **Sensations signs of external objects.** certain objects are presented, certain sensations or states of mind occur to him. These become **signs** of the presence and influence upon him of these several objects. We learn these signs and their significance as we learn the alphabet and the vocabulary of a language; and thus, by experience and habitual practice, come to refer any sensation to some appropriate external object as its cause. This is **Perception.** We are not to suppose that this minute analysis takes place in every act of perception. It is one concrete act, just as in reading we do not analyze each word into its letters and syllables, and think of each elemental sound; but by a glance we comprehend the word, and sometimes the whole sentence, at once.

CHAPTER III.

ACQUIRED PERCEPTIONS.

It must be understood that in the preceding chapter we have given but a bare outline of the philosophy of **Sensation** and **Perception,** and that their relations are not quite so simple as this representation might seem to indicate. Each one of the senses furnishes its very large, diverse, and yet peculiar group of sensations which stand as signs of external facts, the interpretation of which constitutes perception. But these become curiously and wondrously complicated from the fact that each sense borrows from the others. One seems to convey to us knowledge which must have been gained only by another. Thus I find by touch that a certain object is hard, and that another is soft. The one may be a piece of iron, the other a lump of dough. I observe that there is a difference in their appearance. It is probable that we may need a series of experiments in this line before we come to recognize the fact that in a large proportion of soft things there is a certain common appearance to the eye, and that in a large proportion of hard things there is a certain other appearance. We soon learn to distinguish these different appearances, and to associate one with the quality of hardness, and the other with that of softness. Henceforth we distinguish by the eye objects as hard and soft, not always so accurately as

Each sense a borrower from the others.

We learn by experience.

by the touch, and yet for the most part accurately enough

Sight bor-
rowing from
touch.

for practical purposes. So we say of a certain appearance that it has a warm *look*, and of another that it has a cold *look*. Now warm and cold are not qualities that appeal at all to the eye, but we have noticed many times that this appearance of the sky or clouds is accompanied by the one temperature, and that, by the other; hence we use these terms, and are seldom wrong in the qualities they symbolize.

A barrel has another sound if rapped upon when it is empty than when it is full. Hence it is not necessary

Sound bor-
rowing from
touch and
sight.

to ascertain the fact either by sight or by touch, as the sound will give the information sought. So a mason, if he wishes to find whether a wall is solid, can tell by striking here and there with a hammer, and a carpenter will determine where to drive a nail in a plastered wall which has a perfectly uniform appearance to the eye, by rapping with his hammer along the surface till he finds a place which gives a deadened sound. He knows by this that there is a joist behind the lath. In this way, also, do we recognize roughness and smoothness, flexibility and rigidity, solid and fluid substances, and many others by the eye, where the primary means of distinguishing them is by the touch.

Not unfrequently vision has the same effect as physical taste. One is made sick sometimes by the sight

Sight bor-
rowing from
taste.

of some object which is associated with a nauseous odor or flavor. So the sight appropriates as its own what is a matter of judgment, in which, perhaps, several sources of cognition are involved. We learn to estimate distance by the eye. This is gained by a varied process and by considerable experience. We see an object with which we are familiar. We easily determine whether it is near by or far off by its visible appearance. If its outline be clear and distinct, and if it make a certain angle on the eye, we know it is near by. If the outline be somewhat dim and indistinct, and if the visual angle be much smaller than in the other case, we at once decide that it is far off, and we learn to estimate these comparative distances and their measurements by these signs. A butcher or drover who is in the practice of buying cattle by weight, will learn to estimate with marvellous approximation to correctness how much an animal will weigh by simply looking at him.

Distance determined by the eye borrowing from the other senses and faculties.

Weight estimated by sight.

Not only do we learn by the eye what is primarily the product of the other senses, but we very readily apprehend what is directly the product of no sense. We see a blushing cheek, a smiling or frowning face, a downcast expression; all these tell of certain emotions as plainly as we can learn them through any means whatever. Yet certainly emotions are not matters of sensual observation. It is by this mental cooperation, as we might say, of the senses, this service of one to another, of all to each, that we add immeasurably to the number, variety, and wealth of our perceptions. It is probable that our knowledge is many hundred-fold greater than it would be if we were dependent on what each sense, operating by itself and limited to its own natural powers, would give us. This very reasoning suggests to us a certain caution respecting the use of our senses, which may also show us a reason why certain indications that our perceptions are not always valid, are not themselves

States of mind cognized by the eye.

Manifold increase of our knowledge by this co-operation of the senses.

trustworthy. In general, we may say that *the natural and primary perceptions are always valid.* It is

The testimony of our senses valid when original and not borrowed.

only the acquired perceptions that sometimes mislead us. Dr. Wayland relates the story of a person who, on coming to a certain house where he had an appointment, found the door locked; but looking up, he saw what appeared to him to be the key of the door, which he proceeded to take down. On reaching for the key he found there was none there. It was only the painted figure of the key, so shaded as to make the same impression on the eye as a real key would have done. The question arises: Did not his senses deceive him? Is not this an instance of invalid perception? It might appear so. But the latter appearance is no less fallacious than the former. The appearance of the key was false; the appearance of deceit in the sense and perception was also false. Instead of his senses deceiving him, they removed the deception. Instead of his perception apprehending what was not in existence, it was a perception of the real character of the object that set him right and corrected his error. The truth about the matter is, that it was not the primal sense of sight, and the accompanying perception, by which he was misled, but

The acquired perception deceptive, but the primary perception correct.

the *borrowed* or *acquired* perception, the transfer from touch to sight, which did the mischief. The man had associated the particular shades of color then and there appealing to the sense of sight, with a certain form which can only be primarily known through the sense of touch. As soon as the proper sense was brought into requisition, the error vanished.

It is thus also that we are deceived by the appearance

of objects seen in a fog. By our acquired perceptions, as we have seen, we estimate size by distance, and distance by the greater or less distinctness of outline. In a fog, the objects seem farther off than they really are, and we therefore, from our experience in a clear atmosphere, estimate the size accordingly; that is, we estimate the size to be greater than it really is. But this is not from the invalidity of natural and primary perceptions, but from trusting too implicitly to acquired perceptions. Hence it is evident that when our perceptions seem to mislead us, it will generally be found that the error arises, not from our original perceptions, but from those which are acquired.

Objects seen in a fog.

The facility with which, when one sense is destroyed, the other senses acquire means to make up a portion of the deficiency, and the extent to which this can be carried, is worthy of our consideration. We all know how sight supplies the place of hearing in the deaf. Sight, gestures, movements, and facial expressions, instead of sounds, now become symbols of conceptions and thoughts. Not only, thus, does conversation become comparatively easy and rapid between two individuals in the presence of each other, but through the same means, written language is learned, and thus the unfortunate subjects of this deprivation are brought into communication with the intelligent and wise in all ages and places.

In the destruction of one sense the remaining senses become more acute.

So the blind acquire a vastly quicker and larger range of perceptions by means of hearing and touch. It is wonderful how easily a blind man will distinguish pieces of money on which the impressions are only slightly different; how easily he learns

Hearing and touch substituting sight in the blind.

to find his way along streets and lanes, and to houses which he has never seen; to become familiar with the apartments of a house; to know a friend by his voice, or by his tread; to have a thorough understanding of complicated instruments, like pianos and organs, so that he can not only play them, but can tune and repair them, and many other such things. It is related of Laura Bridgman and Julia Brace, both of whom were deaf and blind, that they could distribute the clothes of other inmates of the asylum by the smell, and that one, and I presume both, could converse rapidly with the fingers, could read the books printed in raised letters for the blind, and write very intelligibly.

CHAPTER IV.

NATURE OF THE KNOWLEDGE ACQUIRED BY SENSE-PERCEPTION.

THE knowledge acquired by sense-perception is of **Individuals** and never of **Classes**. We see a tree, a house, an ox, a mountain. We hear a human voice, a bird-song, the bray of a donkey, the roar of the wind, the report of a gun or a cannon. So of the other senses. But let it be carefully noted that we do not think of these several objects as members of classes, though I have used class terms in referring to them. We perceive each of these by itself, and not in any relation whatever to any others as with them constituting groups. How groups or classes are formed will be considered hereafter when we come to the Elaborative Faculties. At present we are concerned about Perception and the nature of the knowledge it gives. This knowledge is only of one and another single object, and by itself would be of only moderate value. *(margin: Knowledge of individuals, not of classes.)*

But precisely *what* do we perceive? It must be remembered that we are now considering Perception, and not knowledge. We see an object before us; we instantly know it to be a horse, or a bush, or a man, or a rock, as the case may be. We commonly use the term Perception for this act of the mind; but evidently if we analyze any such cognitions we shall find some other power or powers of the *(margin: Perception considered by itself, and not as co-operating with other powers.)*

mind involved. The cognition, undoubtedly, is of the concrete, but this cognition, as I have intimated, is made up
of several elements, of which Perception comprises only a part. Perception proper cognizes,
as it seems to me, only qualities or properties.
The mind *knows* by one instantaneous act, of
which Sensation and Perception are elements,
the individual object as a whole. The eye is
affected by the color of an object; there is at the same
instant a perception of an external cause, and a knowledge of the object as colored. The acquired perceptions
give, of course, other particulars concerning the body.
But there is nothing appealing to the senses but certain
qualities. I do not say that nothing else is perceived or
known; because other powers of the mind, as we shall see
later, co-operating with the senses in Perception, give us
full cognition of the individual object.

Perception only one of the elements of cognition.

Cognizes only qualities and not substances.

The qualities which are thus directly cognized by Sense-
Perception have been divided into **primary** and **secondary**.
The **primary** are those which necessarily enter
into our notion of matter; we cannot conceive
of a body which does not possess them. Extension, divisibility, figure, and solidity are some of these.
I have spoken of these as a class of the qualities affecting
the senses. We are told by some writers that these do
not in strict propriety affect the senses at all. They are,
perhaps, all implied in the first, namely, extension; and
extension is by some good authorities regarded as only
the necessary quality attaching to all body, that it must
occupy space. This, it is said, is not given by Perception,
but by the **Pure Reason**, by the very constitution of the
mind. Others, however, take a different view of the

Primary and secondary qualities of matter.

subject, and hold that extension and figure, etc., are given by sight.

The **secondary** qualities are those which are not necessary to our conception of matter, and yet by means of which we are variously affected. Such are smell, taste, sound, color, roughness, smoothness, etc. We can conceive of a body that is not red or yellow; of one that is wanting in a particular odor, or in any odor at all; that is not smooth; but we cannot conceive of a body that does not occupy space, or that does not have some kind of shape. It is true we speak of "shapeless masses," but that is a figurative expression, meaning probably that the shape has no name.

Sir William Hamilton divides the qualities of matter into three classes: first, **primary**; second, **secundo-primary**; third, **secondary**. The primary are objective, not subjective, not sensations proper, but percepts. The secundo-primary are both objective and subjective, percepts proper, and sensations proper. The secondary are subjective, not objective, sensations proper. The **primary** qualities are all deduced from the two necessary ideas of occupying space, and being contained in space. Thus we have, first, extension, divisibility, size, density, and figure; secondly, incompressibility absolute, mobility, situation. *Sir William Hamilton's division of qualities.* *Primary qualities.*

The **secundo-primary** are first, such as result from gravitation, as heavy and light; second, such as are implied in cohesion, as hard or soft, fluid or firm, tough or brittle, rough or smooth, etc.; third, from repulsion result compressible and incompressible, resilient or irresilient; fourth, from inertia we have movable and immovable. *Secundo-primary.*

The **secondary** qualities are subjective affections rather than qualities, in the strict sense ; that is, they are only qualities in the sense that they refer to certain characteristics in bodies which are capable of producing the affection of which we are conscious in ourselves. Such are color, sound, flavor, odor, smoothness, and all the various sensations of physical pleasure or pain which are caused by the peculiarity of bodies. Thus, as has before been noticed in the case of what we call hearing music, we are conscious of a certain state of mind. We learn by experience to refer this state of mind to some outward instrument, or some human voice, as its cause. It is not at all likely that the external object is itself, or that it has in it anything which is identical with, or at all resembles, this state of mind. Nevertheless we have come to believe unhesitatingly that there is something which corresponds to it, and we learn to locate it unerringly.

Secondary.

CHAPTER V.

ATTENTION.

UP to this point the soul has been regarded as scarcely more than the **passive recipient** of impressions made upon it, and the spontaneous interpreter of these impressions. But the mind is an active power, and in the acquisition of knowledge it must be continually putting forth its energies. It is true, the mind must be first affected before it comes into action. But to the calls to action it ordinarily responds with great readiness. When any new state of mind exists, **Attention** is aroused. By this we mean a voluntary directing of the energy of the mind towards an object or act. It has not usually been treated as a distinct faculty, but as a general power of the mind subsidiary to all the faculties. As intimated, it implies action, and is a matter of volition. In the great mass of objects and qualities that come under our observations, we are scarcely, or perhaps not at all, conscious of giving any attention. We pass along the street; we walk without thought, and apparently automatically. That is, the walking seems to do itself. Still we are really paying more attention to our steps than we seem to be. If there is an unexpected obstacle, or a muddy spot, or a rough place, how quickly we observe it, and how readily avoid it, as if we had been on the alert all the while. So during the walk, if in a great city thoroughfare, we meet hundreds of men and women, many of whom we do not seem to see, yet if one of our acquaintances is in the crowd, the readiness with which we recognize him shows that we have been paying some sort of attention to faces all the time.

There is a great variety in the **degrees of attention** which we give to a subject. Sometimes, as has been shown,

Difference in the degrees of attention. there is very little, and yet enough to recognize at once any change in the general view, or any unusual individual in a series. We sometimes, as Dr. Upham says, judge of the degree of attention paid to an object by the length of time one devotes to it. But, as he also says, it is more likely to be the case that we give the more time because our attention is aroused.

There are many people who find it very difficult to fix their attention for any length of time on any one thing,

Difficulties of fixing attention. especially if they have to depend on mere force of will. Many others find no difficulty in giving their attention, if the subject interests them sufficiently. The causes of this interest are various ; curiosity, hope of good news, or even fear of bad news, pleasure in the subject itself, expectation of result in a scientific experiment, and a hundred others. Some persons become so absorbed that everything else vanishes from the mind, and the whole force of the soul bends itself to one point. Mathematicians have been known to solve the most abstruse and complicated problems with every variety and character of disturbance about them. "The man who can fix his attention, without allowing it a single excursion for five consecutive minutes, with or without the schools, is a liberally educated man." [1]

[1] Superintendent Northrup.

It is a question which has been much discussed, whether the mind can attend to more than one thing at a time. Some have strenuously maintained the nega- tive. At one time I so held. But I am now inclined to the opinion that we may have more than one object of thought at a given instant.

Can the mind attend to more than one thing at a time?

It is no doubt true that what sometimes seems to be the presence of two or more simultaneous ideas, is only their rapid alternation. The intense quickness with which the mind acts may leave intervals too small to be discerned, and what appears to be a mere *punctum temporis* may yet be capable of several divisions. It might thus appear possible that

Apparently simultaneous ideas really rapid alternation.

by intensely rapid movement or change the mind may go from one of these infinitesimal intervals to another, or from the thought occurring in one to that in another, in such a way as to make several mental acts appear as one.

But Sir William Hamilton seems to have made it toler- ably clear that the mind must sometimes attend to more than one thing at a time, and that without this view of the subject it is impossible to explain

Hamilton's views.

many phenomena. Thus, for instance, where anything is made up of small parts which must be combined by an action of the mind, as in a picture, these several points must be taken in simultaneously, or the effect is not pro- duced. If it is said we take them all at a time, one disappearing as another appears, and in bringing them together we depend on memory, this would only shift the difficulty. It would be just as much a case of atten- tion to two things if one of the things were a representa- tion of memory as if they were both presentations of

outward or of inward perceptions. It would also, as
Harmony in music. Hamilton thinks, be impossible to comprehend
harmony in music if only one sound were pres-
ent to the mind in the same indivisible instant of time ;
since harmony involves a multiplicity of different tones.
If we resort to memory for an explanation, we have the
same difficulty as pointed out just now in the case of the
picture, only more palpable here. In short, we shall find
that in every case in which judgment, or even comparison,
is called for — and there are few acts of the mind in which
this is not the case — there must be two objects or ideas
present at the same time.

The question arises as to how many things the mind can
attend to at the same time. Sir William Hamilton and
How many things can the mind at- tend to at once? others limit the number to about six as the extreme limit. It is probable that it is only in
rare cases of rare minds that the attention can
be so much diffused. It is probable that it can
be bestowed upon two or three, and sometimes four things
simultaneously. But it is admitted by those who hold this
doctrine that the intensity of the attention is inversely as
the number of objects, — that it would be impossible to
bestow the same amount of attention upon each of three
or four objects simultaneously present as upon one of them
by itself.

There are many illustrations, both of power of concentration which some men have possessed, and of the possible
Remarkable instances of power of concentra- tion. plurality of simultaneous objects of attention.
It is said that Julius Cæsar, while writing a des-
patch, could at the same time dictate four others
to his secretaries, and if he did not write himself,
could dictate seven letters at once. But this was before

the invention of the modern shorthand! Napoleon had the same wonderful power of directing his whole mental energy to one point, and of rapidly shifting it to another.

I have spoken of attention as being **voluntary**, and therefore involving acts of the will. This, perhaps, needs considerable modification. There are undoubtedly very many instances in which attention is involuntary, when it is *compelled* sometimes contrary to the desire of the individual. A vivid flash of lightning, the sudden discharge of a gun near one, any extraordinary spectacle, either attractive by its beauty, or repulsive by its deformity, any unnatural, or perilous, or magnificent, or revolting, object of vision, or event, is likely to command the attention. *[Attention as involving acts of the will. Attention sometimes compelled.]*

For the most part, however, the attention, even when not the result of a direct effort of the will, is so far under the control of the will that it may be withheld from an object towards which it would otherwise spontaneously go forth. But there is also a kind of attention which is the *direct product of the will*. The mind is sometimes compelled by itself to attend to things to which it is naturally averse. Here there is a positive effort of the mind for this purpose. Only minds of unusual power can put forth this effort in certain cases for any considerable length of time. *[But for the most part under control of the will.]*

Hamilton has the following concerning the three degrees or kinds of attention: "The first is a mere vital and irresistible act; the second, an act determined by desire, which, though involuntary, may be resisted by our will; the third, an act determined by deliberate volition." *[Hamilton's three degrees of attention.]*

We have all along been considering attention as the concentration of the mind on some particular object, whether external or internal. Of course it has to do with sense-perception only as the object is external. Some writers have given two different names to the exercise of this power,

Reflection as distinguished from attention.

according as it was directed to objects within or without ; in the former case calling it **Attention,** and in the latter **Reflection.** Others have used the general term Attention in both cases. and have called it Reflection when its objects were internal, and Observation when they were external. But there is no uniformity of usage, and the general term Attention is used for this whole action of the mind, though Reflection, I think, is rarely used, except when we turn our special attention to ourselves ; while Observation is commonly used with reference to both the objective and subjective world. We shall find in other departments of the intellect abundant opportunities for attention in the world of thought, as well as in that of sense.

CHAPTER VI.

THE INNER-SENSE.

THE cognitions and the phenomena we have been considering in the previous chapters are those which pertain to the **world external to the soul,** the world with which we come into communication through the senses. There is another group of cognitions and phenomena Internal totally different from these. The phenomena phenomena. of the soul itself are just as palpable, if not so familiar to the individual, as those of the external world. We have sensations, perceptions, various forms of mental activity, all kinds of pleasures and pains, hope and fear, desire and aversion, pity, contempt, anger, joy and sorrow. We have preferences and choices, determinations and volitions. No one disputes that we know all these phenomena quite as well as, perhaps we may say better than, we know anything in the external world. It is also clear that we Known not by do not know them through the means by which the same means as we we cognize the latter. We cannot hear, touch, know exter- see, smell, or taste a thought or a feeling or a nal things. volition. None of the five senses, nor all of them combined, can apprehend a joy or a sorrow of the soul. They are not necessary cognitions which are given by the constitu tion of the mind itself upon the proper occasions. There must be, then, some other means by which we come into possession of this knowledge.

There is less disagreement among writers concerning

the fact and character of this faculty and its functions,
than about the name. The term popularly used
for this faculty is **Consciousness**, and this has so
strong a position in the custom of speakers and writers that
it is hard to dislodge it. Still there are very few authorities who do not freely admit that this is a restricted use of the term, and that it has a wider
meaning than is here implied. Clearly enough
Consciousness is not confined to any one kind of knowledge,
or to any one group of ideas. It has to do with all knowledge, and, indeed, with all the activities and susceptibilities
of the mind.

The name of this faculty.

This a restricted use of consciousness.

Another term which has been given is **Self-Consciousness**.
This, while avoiding a part of the inconsistency involved
in the preceding term, is still objectionable, from
the fact that Consciousness, whether of self or
of not-self, is not the direct organ or faculty of
any original knowledge, but is the concomitant of all
knowledge and all other mental operations. We
are conscious of no kind of knowledge, only as
that knowledge is given by its appropriate organ,
and it must logically, at least, be given through
some other organ before it is present in consciousness.
Hence we are not conscious of the operations of our minds,
except as we know these in some other manner than by
consciousness itself.

" Self-con-sciousness" criticised.

The concomitant of all knowledge and all mental states.

Another name for this faculty is **Internal Perception**. This
seems to me a very suitable term, and expresses the function
of the faculty very well, only that certain eminent authorities strenuously object to the use
of the term perception in relation to any knowledge, except that received from the external world. I do not see

"Internal perception."

the full force of this objection ; still, as very few make use of this designation, it must for the present be left in abeyance.

The term to which there is the least exception appears to be the **Inner-Sense**. This is not satisfactory, for the reason that it gives us only the name of the faculty, and not of the function it possesses. It has no corresponding adjective. As a sort of antithesis to sense-perception, which is sometimes called the outer-sense, it will answer perhaps better than any other which has as yet been devised.

The "inner-sense" the least objectionable, but not wholly satisfactory.

Of this faculty it may be said, in the first place, that within its sphere it is quite as authoritative as sense-perception. If there be any difference between the two in this respect, it is in favor of the former, because, as already intimated, even in perception our sensations as subjective states are to be tested by the Inner-Sense. If this gives us any reason to doubt concerning the sensation, the doubt will affect the character of our perception. If we can have no absolute certainty from this source, we can have it nowhere. It is our sole reliance in almost the whole study of Psychology. The question of the existence and character of the soul's powers and susceptibilities are to be determined by this faculty.

Of the highest authority.

The sole reliance in psychology.

Much of what we have said concerning **Attention** applies to this faculty and its processes. As in sense-perception, so here, the mind can concentrate itself on a single psychical operation or state, and it is by this operation protracted for a longer or shorter time that some of the most important of mental problems have been solved. The philosophical use of this faculty is one that comes by culture, and it may be increased to a very great extent.

Relation to attention.

It is a question of some importance as to whether the Inner-Sense takes cognizance of all the operations of the

Does the inner-sense take cognizance of all our mental states? mind. This is not the same as whether we are conscious of all our knowledge, since we make a definite distinction between Consciousness in its scientific meaning, and the Inner-Sense. There are good authorities on both sides of the question. There are also facts which seem to bear in both directions. We take the familiar example which almost every person so readily understands. We sit in a room

Sensations produced but not observed. reading, with no disturbing influence; the clock strikes; we take not the slightest note; as we say, it does not attract our attention; apparently it does not affect our mind; the Inner-Sense gives no intimation of any change. Still it is clearly possible that the faculty did take note of the phenomenon. We cannot doubt that the sensation of sound was produced within the mind. To do so would be to deny that the same cause under the same circumstances always produces the same effect. Did, then, the Inner-Sense for some reason fail to cognize the sensation? That it did not, is evident from the fact that when by any means the attention is called to the fact, *not too long afterwards*, there is frequently a vague

Reason for believing that the inner-sense does cognize what it does not particularly notice. and yet not a really doubtful recollection that the clock did strike, and that we heard it; but as our attention was only feebly called towards it, and as the duration of the memory is proportioned to the intensity of the attention, it was almost immediately forgotten. That is the reason why it is only in the cases where the subsequent attention is called very quickly after the event that there is even a vague recollection. Nearly the same thing is true here as in the case of Perception (see pp. 37, 38), where I showed that though it would be naturally presumed that no perception had taken place, yet by comparison with other mental facts we found that such must have been the fact. It is no doubt true that in the action both of the outer and of the inner sense there is actual cognition in many instances when a superficial consideration would indicate there was none. But whether this is so in *all* cases, is not quite so clear.

It is probable, on the whole, that there are states of the mind which are not cognized by the Inner-Sense, but it is also probable that these are not proper objects of knowledge; just as there are conditions of external objects exposed to our senses, which we do not perceive. These may be passive states, perhaps of potentiality, not active nor actual instances of knowing or feeling or willing, of which we are not aware. Take as a single case, memory — what Hamilton calls the retentive element of this faculty. The knowledge of previous facts is said to be retained in the mind. But how retained? It may be that for weeks or months they are not in the mind in the sense of actual knowledge. But the mind has such a relation to them that they may be reproduced when the necessary conditions arise. Then the Inner-Sense cognizes this reminiscent action. Now, there may have been a state of mind indicated by the expression " retained in the mind," of which the Inner-Sense took no note, because it was not a proper object of knowledge. I think there is no act of real knowledge in the mind which is not itself cognized by this faculty. Whether there are other active states of which it is not cognizant, I should hesitate to assert or deny.

[marginal note:] Probably some states of the mind not cognized by the inner-sense.

CHAPTER VII.

CONSCIOUSNESS.

THIS term, as popularly accepted, and as used by many writers, has already been briefly discussed. It has been Popular and seen that, as thus used, it symbolizes only a philosophical small part of what is implied in its complete use of the term. meaning. It no doubt comprises a knowledge of the operations of the soul, but only as it comprises a knowledge of the material world. In neither case does it give these cognitions by itself alone, but only as they are immediately or mediately known in some other way.

There is much difference of opinion among philosophers on this subject. Scarcely any two agree in their treat-Different ment of it, while some are either inconsistent views of in their own statements concerning it, or vague philosophers. and unsatisfactory. Indeed, it would be difficult to find a writer on this subject who has been thoroughly consistent with himself.

" Whatever Consciousness may be, there are three characteristics attributed to it by common consent, and these it must have. The first is, as its etymology, Three char- con-*scio*, implies, it can never be alone. It must acteristics of consciousness always accompany some other operation of the admitted by mind, and does in fact equally accompany all nearly all writers. mental operations. The second characteristic is that it must be infallible. It must be something that never does or can deceive us. In this all are agreed, for, if our consciousness can deceive us, there is nothing between us and universal scepticism. The third characteristic is that consciousness is not a separate faculty. A separate faculty has its own domain, and is subject to the will. It is not a faculty, but is involuntary; it is alike in all the race, and is a necessary concomitant with all mental acts of which we know anything. It has an equal and common relation with all the faculties." [1]

The formula of those who give consciousness the narrower meaning is, "I know that I know." Sir William Hamilton says that consciousness differs from knowledge in this, that in knowledge we know, and in consciousness we know that we know. But if there is need of a separate power to know that we know, we might need an additional power to know that we know that we know, and so on *ad infinitum.* Doubtless we have the fullest assurance possible of our knowledge in the fact that we really know, and in the very act of knowing. Moreover, there is no more need of consciousness to assure us of the knowledge that we know, than of the knowledge that we enjoy and suffer, or that we propose and determine. This is universally admitted. It is also admitted that there is just as much need of such a power to assure us of the knowledge we have of external things, as of the operations of our minds. Sir William Hamilton goes further, and asserts that we are not only conscious of this outward and inward knowledge, but that we are also conscious of the things known, as well as of the fact of knowing them. In

The formula of consciousness in the narrower sense.

Objection to this formula.

Hamilton's doctrine that we are conscious of all the objects that we know.

[1] President Hopkins: Outline Study of Man.

this way he gets the evidence of consciousness for the reality of an external world. I perceive a tree; I am conscious not only of the perception, but I am also conscious of the tree. But, as Dr. Hopkins remarks, "This is to confound consciousness with perception." Any one who would deny the authority of perception would be pretty likely to deny the authority of consciousness.

What, then, is **Consciousness?** Dr. Hopkins again comes to our aid with the most unexceptionable definition I have

Dr. Hopkins's definition.

seen. According to him, consciousness is "*the knowledge of the mind of itself as the permanent and indivisible subject of its own operations.*" [1] This will give

The proper formula.

us the formula of consciousness, not " I know that I know," but, " I know that it is *I* that know, and I know that it is the same I that knows, that also feels and wills." "This knowledge of self as the subject and centre of mental operations will have no reference to the validity or trustworthiness of those operations. We have our faculties. We know by perception, we know by memory. We know immediately, we know mediately; but if our faculty of knowledge, whatever it be, does not suffice to itself, it cannot be supplemented by consciousness. That has another field. It has another sphere. Its

Physical analogy.

office is to bind all the operations of the mind into unity. It does for the mind just what the cellular tissue does for the body. . . . The cellular membrane is found in connection with every part of the body. It infolds, for instance, each fibre of the muscles. It is never by itself. It always accompanies something else, and is for the sake of something else; and it gives unity to the body. And consciousness does the same thing for

[1] Outline Study of Man.

the mind. It is, as it were, its cellular membrane, com-
bining everything connected with it into unity ; A unifying power.
never found by itself, but always present in
connection with every other mental operation. Hence, as
I said, it is not a faculty. It is not under the Not under control of the will.
control of the will. It is not anything that
comes to us in sense or degree through the operation of the will. We have it from the beginning, we
have it by necessity ; one man has it as much as another." [1]

This completes what is essential on the subject of the
Presentative Faculty. It gives us two groups of cognitions : 1. Those that come by **Sense-Perception,** and 2. Those
that are given by the **Inner-Sense.** The former comprise
our knowledge of the external world, or world of matter ;
and the latter, what we know of the internal world, or
world of mind and soul. I have also discussed the topics
of Attention and Consciousness, as being closely, though
not exclusively, related to these faculties.

[1] Outline Study of Man.

PART II.

THE REPRESENTATIVE FACULTY.

CHAPTER I.

THE REPRESENTATIVE FACULTY DESCRIBED.

WE have been hitherto occupied with **Presentative Cognitions**, or cognitions occasioned by the direct presentation of phenomena to the mind. These phenomena, we have seen, are of two classes, **physical** or **material**, and **mental** or **psychical**. They are also given to us through two sets of faculties; namely, Sense-Perception, and the Inner-Sense.

There are many cognitions with which the mind is largely conversant, which come to us through other means than those just described. Some of these are recurrent ideas or conceptions, cognitions re- peated after having been previously present to the mind. Hence they are said to be **re-presented**, and the power through which they are thus brought back is called the **Representative Faculty**. It is defined by Dr. Porter, as "the power to recall, represent, and reknow objects which have been previously known or experienced in the soul." [1] This power to reproduce is evidently a power of the mind itself, and hence, as Dr. Porter says, it essentially involves a creative or self-active power. It will be readily inferred that this power is not limited to the reproduction of sensible or material objects, but embraces as well the acts and products and experiences of the mind itself.

[1] The Human Intellect.

Dr. Hopkins illustrates this tendency to reappearance, of objects once known to the mind, by the figure of a mental current perpetually flowing towards the mind. It is true that this current is not made up exclusively of ideas previously in the mind, since as both the outer and inner senses are active, there will be new cognitions which present themselves along with the representative cognitions. But these latter ideas cannot be excluded in our waking hours, and probably not even when we are asleep. They press somewhat imperatively upon the mind and must be recognized in greater or smaller degree. We may modify the current, we may so treat the cognitions which at any given moment offer themselves, that they shall suggest others than those which would have come in had the train not been interfered with; but the current cannot be stopped.

Dr. Hopkins's "mental current."

An important question here is, whether there are any laws governing this current, or whether the thoughts and conceptions returning to the mind come at haphazard and in no discernible order. Clearly enough they do not come by mere chance, but in a regularly ordered way, and under the direction of laws which it is not difficult to determine. This brings us to the subject of the next chapter.

Laws governing this tendency.

CHAPTER II.

LAWS OF ASSOCIATION.

SAYS Dr. Hickok, " The representatives of former objects of consciousness, when they have fallen, as it were, into the memory, do not lie in this common mental receptacle separately. They are as clusters on the vine, attached one to another by some law of connection peculiar to the case, and which has its general determination for all minds, and its particular modifications for some minds. When one is called up in recollection it does not, therefore, come up singly, but brings the whole cluster along with it. This action of the mind to attach its representatives in the memory one to another is called **Association**, and may include a number of different modes in which such attachments are formed." [1]

Isaac Taylor thus defines Association of Ideas : " If several thoughts, or ideas, or feelings have been in the mind at the same time, afterwards, if one of these thoughts returns to the mind, some or all of them will frequently return with it. This is called **Association of Ideas.**" [2] In other words, the thought or idea that is now in your mind is there probably because a moment ago another thought was there which was some way associated with this ; and the thought which will be in your mind a moment hence will probably be there because of its association with the one now in your mind. I say

Dr. Hickok's statement and illustration.

Definition by Isaac Taylor.

---

[1] Science of the Mind.   [2] Elements of Thought.

probably, because some idea may have been presented through the senses or the Inner-Sense, and thus is not representative. But aside from ideas newly presented, every-

"Sugges-tion." thing that comes back to the mind is suggested, as we say, by some preceding idea. We frequently ask ourselves, " What made me think of that?" plainly implying that we are settled in the opinion that *something*, and clearly something just previously in the mind, was the occasion of the representation of the thought in question.

The Laws of Association are of two kinds, **Primary** and **Secondary**. Of the former, the first in order is **Contiguity of Place**. If, in a certain place, a piece of special good fortune befalls me, or a painful accident occurs, I shall be very likely to recall that incident or experience whenever I revisit that place. This is the reason why special interest attaches to certain places as being associated with events, though not at all interesting in themselves. Plymouth Rock and its immediate surroundings are not in themselves particularly attractive, but thousands every year are drawn to the spot because of the events which took place there two hundred and seventy years ago. The field of Waterloo is a fine piece of agricultural country, which, when I saw it, was covered with bounteous crops, but having nothing of interest in itself to distinguish it from thousands of other farming regions of similar extent. But it is visited by multitudes who associate it with one of the most important events in modern history. It is because of this principle in our constitution that we like to visit the homes of great men of the past. The home of Washington, at Mount Vernon; the house in which Goethe was born in Frankfort; the place where John Huss lodged during his attendance on the Council of Con- stance; the old, and, in itself, very unattractive cottage where Shakespeare first saw the light, —all these are cherished with the profoundest interest by multitudes of persons.

Interest in the homes of great men.

The second of these principles of Association is that of **Time**. Whenever we observe two events transpiring at the same time, and afterwards recall one of them, we are very likely to think of the other. When we meet two persons at the same time, especially if they are somewhat important persons, and perhaps strangers, or partially so to us, and afterwards see one of them alone, we are almost sure to think of the other. It is this prin- ciple that causes us to recall persons and events in groups. If in our reading we come across the name of Pericles, instantly there arise in our minds not only such names as Socrates, Plato, Phidias, Sophocles, Euripides, Themistocles, Aspasia, and Cleon, but many wonderful events of that remarkable period, as well as the glory and grandeur of the famous city where these persons dwelt, and where the events transpired. Hence the value to the student in history, of the habit of fixing in his mind certain great events and personages, each of which is the centre of other events and personages which naturally associate themselves with these. Such a habit will give not only facility but pleasure to the pursuit of this study.

Time.

Why we re- call persons and events in groups.

Importance to the stu- dent of history.

The third of these principles is that of **Resemblance**. When we cognize an object or person or event of any kind which resembles another, we are apt im- mediately to think of that other. This resemblance may

Resemblance.

be merely physical: or it may be mental and moral, that is, of character; or it may be a resemblance of relations instead of qualities and appearances. It is in this way **Formation of types.** that we sometimes form **types.** We say of a remarkable military chieftain, that he is the Napoleon of his age; or of an unselfish and patriotic leader of his people, that he is the Washington of such a nation; or of a certain cataract, that it is a miniature Niagara. This principle is largely effective in metaphor and simile, and other tropical and poetic representations in literature.

The fourth principle is that of **Contrast.** This, though the opposite of resemblance, is closely allied to it as a suggestive principle. We frequently find an idea **Contrast.** which calls up one altogether contrary to it. If we are suffering from cold, we often think of the enjoyment of comfortable warmth. A perception of some deformity leads to the contemplation of objects of beauty. I recollect once hearing a company of singers who were giving an exhibition, and whose music was quite otherwise than attractive or inspiring. I was forcibly reminded of a musical service to which I had not long before listened in the Dresden Cathedral, which was delightful and grand beyond all description. Contrast as suggestive of ideas may be, like that of resemblance, of the outward appearance, or of inward dispositions, or of consequences and results.

Another principle is that of **Cause** and **Effect.** These terms are correlative, and, as such, imply each other. It **Cause and effect.** is one of the most obvious of our mental characteristics, when an event occurs, to inquire the cause, spontaneously and intuitively assuming that there must be a cause. The veriest child is always asking *why* this and that came to pass; that is, inquiring for the **cause,** if it be not obvious. So, too, if we observe any manifestation of power, any conspicuous activity, we naturally think of the effect. Especially is this true when we are familiarly acquainted with the causes or effects of certain observed phenomena. One suggests the other as inevitably as one thing follows another in any naturally arranged order of things. It is in this way that many trains of thought go on in our minds. I see, for instance, in a list of names, that of Martin Luther. I immediately think of the vast series of consequences which followed from his personal influence, the historical events which resulted from his action, the mighty changes wrought in the past, and still in progress. Or I may go back and readily call up the causes which operated to produce this man and fashion his career, and to call forth his reformatory efforts. So of a thousand other incidents in history.

Cause suggests effect.

Means and **End** form another pair of correlatives in thinking of one of which the other is liable to come up in the mind. To think of a locomotive without associating it with the moving of a train of cars, of a dam without the detention of water to form a head or power, or to conceive of a foundation aside from the edifice resting upon it, is scarcely possible.

Means and end.

These six principles of Association appear to be sufficient to account for all the phenomena involved. Certain writers have added others, as follows: Objects or events produced by the same power suggest one another and the power concerned. The sign and the thing signified are so closely associated in the mind that ideas of the one are likely to be followed by those of the other, and *vice versa.* Objects accidentally designated by the same

These principles of association sufficient to account for all the phenomena of representation.

sound operate in the same way, and thus the amusement that many persons get out of the not very refined practice of punning. But probably each of these latter principles can be brought under one or another of those previously given. On the other hand it has been claimed that these principles can be reduced to a smaller number than those given in detail. A considerable portion of the writers on Psychology agree in putting them all in three groups ; namely, Time and Place, Cause and Effect, Resemblance and Contrast. Others have reduced them to two : Affinity and Simultaneity. Some high authorities teach us that they may all be comprehended under one ; namely, the law of Redintegration. This is expressed in the formula that "a part of a mental state tends to bring back and restore all the parts that compose it." Dr. Porter, while admitting that most of the principles of association which we have spoken of as treated separately can be brought under this law of Redintegration, yet shows that it is at least exceedingly doubtful in some cases. For instance, in the case of resemblance, the parts which are assumed as parts of the same whole are not identical parts, but similar parts, and hence will not allow of Redintegration. As, for instance, when we see a horse, and then on seeing another horse we observe some feature in the latter which resembles a corresponding feature in the former. This calls up the horse previously seen. But that which calls up this absent object is not some part of it, but a resemblance of that part, which semblance is yet a part of another and not of the same.

Dr. Porter proposes to bring these principles all under

Possible reduction of these six principles to a smaller number.

Dr. Porter's objection.

one law of another kind, which he thus states : "The mind tends to act again more readily in a man-ner or form which is similar to any in which it has acted before, in any defined exertion of its energy." This statement is obviously true, but it is doubtful if it accounts for all the phenom-ena of association.   For instance, as Dr. Hopkins says, " I see in it no more reason why, if I pass the place where I met a friend yesterday, I should think of him then and there, than at any other time and place. If the tendency be there, independent of circum-stances, it would be as likely to show itself at one time as another; but if it depends on circumstances, we are thrown back upon the original law, having simply that and whatever tendency may be implied in our having a representative faculty at all."

Tendency of the mind to act in a way similar to a former action.

Dr. Hop-kins's ob-jection.

We have so far been speaking of the **Primary Principles** of Association.   There are also **Secondary Principles**.   Ac-cording to these, ideas and objects tend to sug-gest one another in proportion as the following conditions exist.   1. The vividness with which objects are presented to the mind affects the readiness of their recurrence.   Some events possess little or no inter-est for us.   These would not be readily repro-duced.   Others, as a piece of unexpected good news, or some startling phenomena, come back more easily and more clearly.   How often do we hear persons, describing some unusually exciting occurrence or very impressive event. say. "I shall never forget it so long as I live ! "

Secondary principles of associa-tion.

Vividness of original presenta-tion.

2. Events more recent are more apt to return to the mind.   Thus what we have seen or heard within a day or

two is more likely to recur to us than the same kinds of

Recent events.

events which took place six months or a year ago. This and the preceding principle, however, it will easily be seen, modify each other. The greater vividness often makes up for the lapse of time, and so sometimes an occurrence of yesterday is forgotten where

Why aged persons recall events of their youth, but not those more recent.

one of a month or a year ago is distinctly recalled. It is in this way that we account for the fact that aged persons recall with remarkable distinctness experiences of fifty or sixty years ago, while they are totally oblivious of events of the same importance which transpired within a month or even a week. The reason of this is that in our earlier years our minds are more impressible, while in old age both our faculties and our susceptibilities become dulled and the impression of the same event is vastly less in the latter case than it would have been in the former.

3. Frequent repetition of an experience, whether of observation or of some subjective action tends to promote

Frequent repetition.

its easy recurrence. This is the reason why it is profitable for young pupils to go over their tasks frequently in preparation for their recitations, and why reviews are essential in order to prepare one for examinations.

4. Peculiarities of mental character have much to do with the readiness or otherwise with which certain pre-

Peculiarities of mental character.

vious states of the mind reappear. We are differently constituted, and that, too, in many respects. Some have an aptitude for mathematical studies, others have a taste for philosophy and science, others still are characterized by predominance of æsthetic sentiment, and others tend towards the practical. It is

said of one man who had read Milton's "Paradise Lost,"
that he didn't think it of much value, as it *proved* nothing.
Wordsworth says, —

> "To me, the meanest flower that blows can give
> Thoughts that do often lie too deep for tears."

While of the clown the same poet says, —

> "A primrose by a river's brim,
> A yellow primrose was to him.
> And it was nothing more."

We can readily see that with minds differing so widely and
so variously in predispositions, tastes, and aptitudes, there
must be a correspondingly wide difference in the character
of the associations, and consequently of the mental current.

5. In general, whatever tends to fix the attention, whether
in any of the ways previously mentioned, or in
any other way, will affect the order and determine the manner of representation.

Any power to fix the attention.

We can by no means always trace the causes of successive suggestions by which any given subject reappears in
the mind at a given time. We frequently find
ourselves dwelling on a topic, and we are somehow led to ask ourselves, "How did we come to
think of this?" It may be that by careful effort we are able
to discern the occasion of its coming, and that, too, when
at first it may appear to have come causelessly. But in
other cases, search as diligently as we may, we cannot de-
tect the slightest connection between the present thought
and any previous one. This probably arises from the fact
that the subject which suggested the one noticed was too
unimportant or evanescent to attract the attention, and be
retained by the memory, though sufficient to form a connect-
ing link in the series. It vanished from the mind as soon

Difficult to trace the causes of suggestions.

as it arose, and was quickly crowded out of consciousness by thoughts of greater importance. Sir William Hamilton, as we have seen, would regard many of these links as mental acts or states of which we are unconscious. But this seems hardly necessary.

We have been speaking of these principles of Association as **Laws**, — natural laws, — and as such there must be in them a large element of necessity. So far as this is the case, the order of our thoughts in representation is not subject to the free action of the mind. Still we are conscious of a power at least partially determining their order. It therefore becomes a matter of some interest to inquire how far and in what manner the mind, can influence the order of representation. In the first place, it can have no direct influence. Obviously enough the mind cannot choose what idea or object shall present or represent itself to the mind, for the simple reason that such choice cannot be made unless the objects among which the choice is to be made are already present to the mind. Hence the order must be determined previously by some other power than that of the mind. There are natural laws in accordance with which the representation takes place, and there are causes operating which belong to our constitution, and which are not implied in the voluntary action of the mind.

These principles are natural laws.

How far and in what manner can the soul influence the order of representation?

Still, the mind has a certain power over the current or train of thought, affecting it *not directly*, but *indirectly*. While certain thoughts will, independently of the mind's action, present themselves, it is competent for the mind to meet them at the threshold and give its attention to certain of these

The mind has an indirect power of control or modification.

rather than others, and so detain some for special consideration, while others pass on into oblivion. By thus detaining a certain idea and looking at it more particularly, this very process may call up new objects and trains of thought, which would never have come but for this voluntary action of the mind. Thus there may, in the natural order, occur to me a thought of Bunker Hill; this may suggest to me the monument there, and this, Webster's oration at the laying of the corner-stone, and this the career of the great orator and statesman, and this lead off to other orators and men of powerful intellect. Or I may detain the idea of the first suggestion instead of letting my mind run on spontaneously, and may by force of will compel myself to attend to the event the monument was designed to commemorate, the fierce battle, the encouragement which the stubborn and effective resistance gave men in defeat, and thus follow the whole history of the war, or any portion of it, till some other incident presents itself upon which I may think fit to dwell. In this way we may come to have great control over our thoughts, and turn them to higher or lower meditations, as we please. Of course, to be always pursuing a profitable and wholesome line of thought requires effort and much culture, but we so fully recognize this as practicable that we do not hesitate to condemn a man who lets his mind run perpetually on low and unworthy themes, or to commend one who has habituated himself to elevated and wholesome thinking. We can also, by foresight and moderate skill, determine the associations which decide what our trains of thought shall be. This, much more than we can estimate, has to do with the style of men or women we shall be, and the kind of characters we shall have.

Effort and discipline required to do this effectually.

CHAPTER III.

THE FORMS WHICH THE REPRESENTATIVE PRODUCT ASSUMES.

THERE are *three forms* which Representation assumes in the mind ; namely, **Fantasy**, **Memory**, and **Imagination**.

By **Fantasy** is meant the power which the mind has of forming images of objects which have been previously pre- **Fantasy defined.** sented to it, these images being wholly severed from all relations of time and place. It is this latter feature which distinguishes it from Memory, to which the time element is essential. It is distin- **How distin- guished from memory and imagination.** guished from Imagination in that the latter is constructive and in a sense creative. It is also less under the control of the will, and is not subject to judgment nor guided by taste. It is the characteristic of undisciplined minds, or of those relaxed and freed from restraint, though not confined to these. It is active in reverie, and becomes predominant in disturbed sleep or half-waking conditions, in dreams and somnambu- **Images come and go spon- taneously.** lism ; as also in children and savages. In all these conditions here implied, the images come and go more or less and sometimes entirely at random and hap-hazard, frequently in utter chaotic confusion and with the strangest mixture of elements. The term **fantastic** both etymologically and appropriately expresses many of the products of this form of representation. Sometimes under the influence of certain bodily conditions the representations are most disagreeable and painful; but sometimes also they are just the opposite.

The word **Fancy** is in its origin a synonyme of Fantasy. But recently and in its more popular use it has a some- what wider range, and in philosophy it has a Fancy and meaning somewhat distinct from that just now fantasy. assigned to Fantasy. But the terms are not radically dif- ferent. Fancy "collects materials for the Imagination; therefore the latter presupposes the former, while the for- mer does not necessarily suppose the latter." [1] Whether Fantasy or Fancy, it is a power by which images of indi- vidual objects formerly perceived are re-presented to the mind, usually without perceptible effort of the Words- will. Wordsworth says, Fancy "does not re- worth's quire that the materials she makes use of should statement. be susceptible of change in their constitution from her touch; and where they admit of modification, it is enough for her purpose, if it be slight, limited, and evanescent."

MEMORY.

It is one of the facts with which all are familiar, that the mind has the power to retain cogni- The mind's tions of which it has come into possession power to — or, as it may be more fully stated, the mind retain cog- nitions. has the power of returning to states in which it has formerly been, with a clear consciousness that they are recurrences of former states. It is held by not a few writers of note, that no cognition, or thought, or feeling, or mental action of any sort which has ever existed, can ever so far be lost as that it may No cognition not under certain conditions recur. We do wholly lost. certainly know that a very great number of our mental

[1] Dugald Stewart.

experiences return to us, and that too sometimes, when, owing to their trivial character, or the long lapse of time, it would seem most unlikely. This characteristic of the mind we call **Memory**.

There are two functions of Memory; namely, **Conservation** or **Retention**, which has in part been already described,

Two func-
tions of
memory.

and which Sir William Hamilton regards as Memory proper, and **Reproduction**; Hamilton adds also Representation. But Representation is a generic term including not only Conservation and Reproduction, but all kinds of recurring mental experiences.

Reproduction is either *spontaneous* or *voluntary*. In both

Reproduc-
tion of two
kinds.

cases it proceeds under the laws of Association. **Spontaneous Reproduction** is when the previous thought recurs to the mind through the operations of the general laws of Association, without effort or

Spontaneous
reproduc-
tion distin-
guished from
fantasy.

volition on the part of the subject. It is distinguished from Fantasy only by the recognition of the element of time, that is, of the fact that the state of mind has been previously experienced.

Voluntary Reproduction or **Reminiscence** occurs when an effort is made to recall some thought or cognition of the

Voluntary
reproduc-
tion.

past. Every one is familiar with the fact that frequently when we have a part, or some intimation, of a former presentation in mind, we seek to reproduce the whole; as, for instance, having distinctly in mind a person or place, we endeavor to recover the name, which has escaped us, and which, as we say, we have *forgotten;* or knowing the name, possibly, we strive to bring back the object. This we do by compelling certain associations which if left to themselves would take another direction; or by concentrating the

mind upon certain suggestions when others would occur
if left to spontaneity. In the one case we follow the general connection existing among associated ideas and the
line of easy and natural suggestion; in the other by an
energetic effort we select such associations as are likely to
lead to the recognition desired. This is commonly called
Recollection, as in it we re-collect the missing elements
which make up the entire representation. Of
course, it is obvious that we cannot recall that
Recollection.
of which the mind has no knowledge whatever. When,
for instance, I try to recall a name of which the object is
already present to my mind, or an object of which the
name is present, I already know that there *is* a name or an
object, as the case may be. There is always something
some way related to that which we desire to recall, and
from this the association must proceed.

VARIETIES OF MEMORY.

There are wide *differences* in the memory of different
individuals. These differences are in respect of both kind
and power. Some remember *words* and *names*
with great facility, others retain these but feebly,
Instance.
while they recall *things* readily. One man will easily recognize a face he has once seen or a person he has previously
known, while it is with great difficulty he can recollect the
name. Another class of persons retain and reproduce circumstances and events with remarkable accuracy and
minuteness. The last is likely to be the case with uneducated persons. Such a memory has been called
Circumstantial. Others still have a logical or
Circumstan-
tial memory.
scientific memory. They recall the thought or principle
connected with the object, and thus recollect the latter.

This difference depends much upon the habit and character of association which one cultivates. The peculiarities of the several laws of association are also seen here. This is the case, especially, in the difference between circumstantial and logical memory. Uneducated people, not having the mind trained to systematic thinking, naturally associate objects and events by the contiguity of time and space. They are likely to take in many concomitant particulars. In a representation of their reminiscences to others this often has a picturesque effect, but oftener it becomes tedious, diverting the attention from essential points. The opposite is the case with philosophic minds. They seize upon the reality rather than the appearance, upon the thought rather than its embodiment. It has frequently been noted that while in the former case the memory is more ready, in the latter it is slower but more sure and confident.

Logical memory.

It is more difficult to determine the cause of a purely verbal memory. It is not impossible that the principle of association here is that of time and place. The sound of the word — less likely, its written form — is associated with the person or thing, and their association is more intense from the fact that there is no thought or principle to absorb any part of the mind.

The variations in the *power* of memory are still more striking. We have instances of extraordinary tenacity which would be incredible were they not well authenticated. It is related that Themistocles knew every citizen of Athens, and that Cyrus could recognize every soldier of his great army. Hortensius, it is said, could sit all day at an auction, and at evening could give an account from memory of every-

Variations in the power of memory.

thing sold, the purchaser, and the price.　In modern times
we have equal feats of the memory.　Dr. Waller　<small>Extraordi-</small>
of Oxford on one occasion, at night, in bed, pro-　<small>nary in-</small>
posed to himself a number of fifty-three places,　<small>stances.</small>
and found its square root to twenty-seven places, and,
without writing down the number at all, dictated the result
from memory twenty days afterward.　"The librarian of
the Duke of Tuscany would inform any one who consulted
him, not only who had directly treated of any particular
subject, but who had indirectly touched upon it while treat-
ing of any other subject, to the number of perhaps one
hundred and fifty authors, giving the name of the author,
the name of the book, the words, often the page where they
were to be found, and with the greatest exactness.　It is
said that a gentleman of Florence lent him a manuscript
which he had prepared for the press, and some time afterward went to him with a sorrowful face, pretending to have
lost his manuscript by accident, and begging the librarian
to recall what he could of it and write it down.　He immediately set about it, and wrote out the entire manuscript,
without missing a word.　At one time the Grand Duke
sent to him to inquire if he could procure a certain book
which was very scarce.　'No, sir,' said the librarian ; 'there
is but one copy in the world, that is in the Grand Seignior's
library in Constantinople, and is the seventh book on the
seventh shelf, on the right hand as you go in.'"

It has been a largely prevalent opinion that great strength
of memory is incompatible with a high degree of　<small>Powerful</small>
intellectuality.　This is clearly an error.　There　<small>memory com-</small>
<small>patible with</small>
have been persons of extraordinary memory who　<small>high intellec-</small>
have had, at the same time, only moderate in-　<small>tuality.</small>
telligence and slender resources in the way of　thought.

This is especially true in some marked instances of verbal memory. But to leap from these isolated facts to the general conclusion that a good memory necessarily implies feeble intellectual action, is very poor reasoning. Scaliger, Grotius, Pascal, Leibnitz, Euler, Macaulay, and Hamilton, and a thousand others, each possessed an extraordinary memory, and were at the same time men of the greatest intellectual power. Let no student neglect any means of cultivating a good memory, under the impression that it will unfavorably affect his other faculties.

Instances.

CULTIVATION OF THE MEMORY.

There is no doubt that the power of the memory can be greatly increased. It may also be impaired by neglect or misuse. I have not much faith in mnemonic systems. They are too artificial, and it has sometimes seemed as if it required more outlay of mental energy to learn the system than to remember the facts and principles which it is presumed such a system aids in recalling. Of late such devices have not been much in vogue. Just now, however, a new interest has sprung up in respect to means of cultivating the memory, which are supposed to promise valuable results. What the outcome will be, remains to be seen.

Mnemonic systems.

But aside from these adventitious aids there are certain practical rules by which the memory itself may be essentially improved. The chief of these are as follows : —

Rules for improving the memory.

1. **Trust the Memory.** It is believed by many that the memory of the ancient was much greater than that of the modern scholars. The reason assigned is not unnatural. Books were far less numerous then

Trusting the memory.

than now. For this reason, men were compelled to rely on their memory. Like some other powers of the mind, the more we demand of it the more freely and fully does it respond. It is true, however, that the memory may be overtaxed and thus impaired. For this reason trivial and useless things may be dismissed, or, at least, less effort should be made to retain them.

2. The memory becomes more retentive as we give more **Careful and Discriminating Attention** to the subject under consideration. We do not readily recall those Careful attention. things of which we do not have a clear apprehension. Hence the necessity of close and minute observation. Any one who notes particularly the habits of students finds that in a very large proportion of the instances in which one is unable to recall what he supposes himself to have learned, it is because he has failed to get a good understanding of the matter. In some cases which have come under my own observation the defect even arose from the fact that the learner was a poor reader. Many, especially among young students, — and we may well wish it were confined to them — fail to get on with their studies simply because of their careless and slovenly habits of reading. They do not fairly take in the essential thoughts represented on the printed page.

3. By **Wise Habits of Association.** This implies the power and practice of thorough analysis. There will naturally follow from this the grouping of particulars in Association. logical and systematic order about general principles. This is essential to the command of many and complicated elements. For instance, a person may go into a large library knowing nothing about it Systematic order. but the fact that there are ten or twenty or

fifty thousand volumes. He may look at a hundred different books and spend hours in doing so. But, take

Illustration. whatever pains he may, he will carry away only
a chaotic impression of a multitude of printed
works, and nothing at all of the essential character of the
collection. But let him know beforehand that these are
arranged according to some general principle — it may be
logical or geographical — let us suppose the former ; he
now sees that in one alcove are placed all the mathematical treatises under their various subdivisions ; in another
all the historical works ; in another those on Natural Science under the several heads of Physics, Natural History,
Mineralogy, Chemistry, etc.; and in still others Metaphys-
ics, Theology, Law, Physics, and Literature ; if he has
paid any considerable degree of attention to their classification, he carries away an intelligent conception of the
character of the library, and will be able to convey it to
others.

It is thus, by a proper and sensible discipline of the
memory, that men become able writers ; not by thinking

Relation to
writing and
extempora-
neous speak-
ing. over a disconnected jumble of thoughts which
they would like to present to others, but by
classifying and systematizing these, so that the
mind can command them. This, too, is the
power of memory which is essential to the extemporane-
ous speaker. There are men whom we know who can
speak two hours or more without notes, holding thousands
with unflagging interest, not because they have memorized
their topics, much less their words, but because they have
so arranged their thoughts, that under the laws of association they naturally suggest one another, and so present
themselves in the order in which they are wanted. A

good memory, then, is not to be estimated at a low value, but as one of the greatest of our intellectual powers.

Most persons realize in only a small degree **the Importance of Memory.** All who reflect will see at once how inconvenient it would be if we had no memory, and what an advantage it is to carry along in our mind the knowledge of many past events and experiences. But Memory is very much more than a convenience. It is absolutely essential *Importance of memory not fully realized by many persons.* to a very large proportion of all the operations of the intellect. Without Memory we could not reason, we could scarcely judge; we could not converse; we could not carry on mathematical or scientific investigations; reading would be useless to us, *Relation to reasoning and judgment.* not merely as failing to be retained, but as failing also to give us even present information and entertainment. Business could not be transacted. The most ordinary workman must remember what he is *Reading.* to do and how to do it; what he has already done and its relation to what is to be done, and a thousand other minute and apparently utterly unimportant items which nevertheless are essential to be *Business.* kept in mind in the simplest undertaking. It is the keystone of the intellectual arch, and without it, with all the other great powers of the soul, we should be scarcely more than the merest idiots.

IMAGINATION.

This is the third of the forms which Representative Cognition takes. It may be defined as *the power to recombine materials already in the mind, into new wholes.* The difference between it and Fantasy *Imagination defined.*

has already been indicated. The difference between it and Generalization, or the formation of concept, is that in the latter case we form groups of objects just as they exist in nature and unite them by one or more similar qualities. But in Imagination we combine the several elements, not into a group of individualities, but into a single mental individual, different from any one thing that is found in nature, — a product of the mind itself. The Imagination is a more positive force than either Fantasy or Memory, and more directly under the control of the will. It is, in an important sense, a creative power. It is not, as the word might seem to indicate, a mere image-making capability. As Dr. Hickok says, "The sense-constructions are properly images; but they are products of the Fancy, and not of the Imagination, which has higher and more complex work in hand."

A creative, not a mere image-making power.

Imagination is of **two grades**. It may either simply recombine the materials furnished into new forms, or it may form ideals, intimations of which exist in perceptions or representations already before the mind, and actualize them in new constructions. Thus a painter whose imagination is of the former grade may, from a number of beautiful faces, select such features of each as will answer his purpose, and combine them into a picture which will be like no one of them, but which will be more beautiful than any of them. This is an instance of the former and lower order of this faculty. It is little better than mechanical piece-work, and never comes up to the character of art in its proper sense.

Two grades.

In the other kind of Imagination there is something more than recombination in the ordinary sense of that term. There are conceptions of new features suggested, doubtless, by those already existing, as being fit complements of them in the structure contemplated, or desirable supplements. Thus in architecture, for instance, when the artist begins to plan his building, there are present to his mind many buildings whose general purpose is the same as that which he is to design. But as he arranges the parts of the intended structure he thinks that a certain feature, not found *The higher kind of imagination. Suggestions of new features.* in any of the others which he has seen, would add to its beauty and convenience; and he puts it in his plan, at first perhaps tentatively, and, after much modifying and shifting of positions and relations, settles upon its final arrangement as a part of the whole. This may be repeated in a variety of cases in the same building until the whole takes on a unique and original form, more admirable than anything which he has previously seen. The same process may characterize the painting of a picture, or the writing of a poem, or the composition of a piece of music. In the case of genius or even of a high order of talent, we thus have what is regarded as an original piece of work, something in which not only the general effect is new and surprising, but each part seems to have been made for its particular relation to the whole.

A striking illustration of this kind of Imagination may be found even in **Mechanical Invention**. Few probably are aware how large a part Imagination plays here. Take, for instance, a mowing machine, or a machine for making mill-cards, or any other *Its office in mechanical invention.* similar piece of mechanism. No one of these is constructed by taking parts of other machines and merely forming a new combination better than any of them. It is a new invention altogether. True, it may be of gradual develop-

ment, and it may be a long time coming to perfection. But usually the first contrivance is something wholly different from anything previously devised. Possibly the inventor
How the new structure may be sug- gested. is first moved by the desire for some more rapid way of gathering the grain, or making the cards, than the old, slow method by hand. Or, possibly, before any such desire has consciously risen in his mind, some accident suggests to him a means of diminishing the labor, or of more easily and rapidly accomplishing the work. He spends much time in thinking about it, but this thinking is always accompanied by an active Imagina-
How imagi- nation works here. tion. Little by little the instrument forms itself in his mind. At first it is only a part, perhaps a small part, of what will be needed to accomplish after a moderate fashion what he proposes to effect with the new machine. But in quiet hours, perhaps of the night, when other men sleep, he imagines the whole thing, so far as it has progressed, in his mind, and works upon it there, rearranging and reconstructing it. He puts in an additional wheel, or takes out a superfluous one; supplies a lever in one place, or a cog somewhere else; and calculates how it will work, or whether it will work at all. The point here is, that at present it is a thing of the Imagination; it is wholly in his mind, and he works upon it as a reality, while as yet it has no outward form.
Its embodi- ment. At length, when he thinks it somewhere nearly complete, he ventures on its embodiment in iron and brass and wood and leather, and is ready for actual experiment with it. It may prove a failure, but it is certainly not always that, for we have hundreds of these children of the brain doing multifarious service in the productive industries of the world.

What I wish to show here is that Imagination, and that of the higher order, is involved. Doubtless a combination of material in new forms is also implied, but there is something incalculably more than this. The material in such cases exists in more or less approximately primitive forms, and the combination is of a kind that implies original powers far beyond that of the lower order first mentioned. *Something very much more than the recombination of materials.* While the product of the higher forms of Imagination is not creative in the extreme sense of that term, it is in the popular and more common sense. It is not a modification or combination of products previously existing, but it is to all practical intents an entirely new formation. *Not creative in the extreme sense, yet it is in the ordinary sense.*

It is not to be understood by what has just been said, that Imagination is either wholly or in part synonymous with **Invention**. They are distinct powers of the mind. The latter has reference usually to the production of something actual, while the former deals entirely with the ideal. *Not synonymous with invention.* Still they are closely associated, and neither operates in any way of large efficiency without the aid of the other. Even in the ideal constructions with which the mind is sometimes busy, invention occasionally plays an important part. While, on the other hand, in the great inventions of industrial art, the Imagination is an indispensable agent.

CHAPTER IV.

RELATION OF THE IMAGINATION TO SOME OTHER FACULTIES.

Memory and **Imagination** are alike in this respect, that they are both forms of **Representation.** But the former Memory and gives us objects as they actually were at some imagination. previous time; the latter has to do with ideal objects. The former deals with the past; the latter has no temporal limitations, — it disports itself alike in the past and in the future.

Judgment differs from Imagination in that the former deals with the relations of things, and also that it has to do principally with *actual* relations; while the lat-Judgment. ter, as we have seen, deals wholly with ideals. Judgment has specific reference to truth, and nothing is really either true or false except Judgments, or, as they are called when expressed in language, propositions. But Imagination is not limited to what is true or real; it extends itself to all that is possible or conceivable. Still a good Imagination is always accompanied by a sound Judgment. What is fitting and proper; what will best convey the ideas in the mind; or what will most correctly and properly fill out the representation, — these are largely matters of Judgment. The products of the Imagination are often much at fault from the lack of good Judgment on the part of the agent.

Reasoning is to a certain extent subsidiary to, and affiliated with Imagination, but is clearly distinct from it. Like Judgment it has largely to do with truth and fact, while Imagination deals with possibilities and conceptions. Reasoning proceeds from established premises; but Imagination has no need of these. Still reasoning is not wholly alien to the work of Imagination, but has some subsidiary relation to it. In forming out of the materials in hand the combination desired, it is pretty nearly certain that there will be occasion for drawing inferences as to proportion, situation, or symmetry, or some other condition of the new whole, or all of these.

Reasoning.

Taste is closely connected with Imagination, while yet not at all identical with it. The latter may exist in high degree where the former is greatly deficient, if not wholly wanting. But taste is essential to the best effect of the Imagination. Without it, the latter will become wild, grotesque, and offensive. This is especially the case when beauty is the aim in any department of representative art. Taste must regulate and direct the Imagination. Together with the Judgment it is an essential guide and modulator of this power of the mind.

Taste not identical with, but closely related to, imagination.

ACTIVE AND PASSIVE IMAGINATION.

This is a division made by some writers, but not admitted by others. Whatever may be the difference of opinion, it must have reference rather to the designation than to the matter of fact. There can be little doubt that somewhat of a distinction is to be made. It is certain that while some persons have the power to originate pictures and representations of remarkable

Some distinction certain.

effectiveness, others who cannot do this, yet can re-form these when presented to the mind, and can appreciate the representation when thus made. Only a few persons have the former power, while a great many have the latter; there are also a smaller number who have it in only a slight degree, or possibly not at all. It certainly requires some Imagination to appreciate a picture of real merit, or a group of statuary evincing much ability on the part of the artist, or a poem, or even a good dramatic story; and hundreds have this capability where perhaps only one could represent any of these.

CHAPTER V.

UTILITY OF THE IMAGINATION.

MANY persons are disposed to regard Imagination as having no real **utility**, or, at least, none for the more serious purposes of life; they would treat it as at the best wholly ornamental. But even if this were true, it would not necessarily follow that it had no utility. Use and beauty are not wholly alien to each other, nor are they mutually antagonistic. A thousand things are useful simply because they are beautiful. Otherwise it would appear that the all-wise Creator had put a vast amount of useless work into the structure of the physical universe. It would probably not be very difficult to prove that many things are beautiful just because of their utility. And this, too, by no excess of figurative language. But even if the allegation were true that there is such an antagonism, still we should find on examination that Imagination has an important office among the utilities of humanity.

In the first place, Imagination is often essential to the writer or speaker in setting forth what he wishes to convey to the minds of others. No man can so describe a scene or a series of events as to produce the desired effect on those who hear him, unless he is possessed of a certain degree of Imagination. Hence an orator, an essayist, a teacher, a historian without this

Imagination often regarded as without utility, and merely ornamental.

Use and beauty not antagonistic.

Many things beautiful by reason of their utility.

Imagination useful to writers and speakers.

faculty would be, if not a failure, at least greatly lacking in effectiveness. This is one of the principal differences between an eloquent orator or writer, and one that is dull and uninteresting, though perhaps equally intelligent and learned — the former brings his subject vividly before our minds simply because he has a vivid conception of it himself, and is able to give us such outlines and points of the picture that it easily reproduces itself in the minds of those to whom it is presented; the other gives a dry detail of facts or principles or arguments, which commends itself to only a few minds.

Difference between an imaginative and an unimaginative speaker or writer.

We have already seen something of the mutual relations of Imagination and Invention. It would be nearly impossible for a man, no matter what his genius in other respects, to devise a complicated machine if he had no Imagination. Very often the whole structure must be imagined first in his mind and must there be held subject to various modifications, before even a draught of it is made, to say nothing of a model.

Successful invention impossible without imagination.

So, too, in great practical enterprises, plans must be formed in the mind, and, so to speak, be manipulated there, before they can be projected in actualities, or even described and published. Napoleon in arranging for one of his great campaigns, reaching through months of time, and extending over many leagues of territory, and comprising all the divisions and subdivisions of an army of a hundred thousand men, with all the immense trains of artillery and baggage, — wishing to keep the matter secret till the time arrived to begin to carry it into execution, held the whole plan in his own mind. Each day's march of each division and the

Business enterprises.

Instance of Napoleon.

different routes, the points of convergence and concentration, the time and place where the first battle would probably be fought, the subsequent movement in different
lines, the concentration again, the time and place of the
second battle, and all the complicated operations, many of
them depending upon many contingencies; yet all these
calculated with wonderful skill and marvellous prescience
— were carried in his head till the hour to divulge them
came. Then he called his chief of staff, and in a rapid,
conversational manner, gave an exposition of the whole
plan and had it put on paper as he gave it out. It is said
that the actual movements throughout, notwithstanding
the natural uncertainty of battles of which there were
several, and the fortuities which no human mind could
anticipate, corresponded almost entirely with the conceptions previously formed in the mind of the great captain.
It may be said that there were other powers than that of
the Imagination involved here. True ; but it is impossible to suppose that a man either destitute of this power,
or possessing it only in a low degree, would be competent
to form and carry in his mind so gigantic a plan.

Even in science it is not possible to dispense altogether
with this faculty. Very much of our modern
scientific investigation involves **Hypothesis**, and
at least an important faculty in the formation of
hypothesis is Imagination. The Imagination was as really
concerned in the hypothesis of Ptolemy and in
that of Copernicus relating to the movement of
the heavenly bodies, as in Michael Angelo's " Moses " or
Milton's "Paradise Lost." In many of the minor sciences
its utility is not the less great.

But Imagination is of especial value in the formation of

ideals of excellence in every department of human interest.

Formation of ideals. Ideals are representations of that which we regard as perfect, and they are solely the creatures of the Imagination. As set before us they are higher than anything we have yet attained to — higher perhaps Meaning of ideals. than anything really attainable — but as conditions at which we aim and towards which we may, more or less, approximate, they are of untold advantage. This is particularly the case in respect to conduct Value in respect to character. and character. The man who places before him the ideal of a pure and lofty character, delighting in it, as he must, if he forms it at all, almost unconsciously strives to realize it in his own life. The person who does not have some such ideal is not likely to make much of his life. He simply drifts about exposed to winds and currents which carry him whither they will; he lives a purposeless life, and attains to no high excellence.

CHAPTER VI.

CULTIVATION OF THE IMAGINATION.

THIS faculty, like all other powers of the mind and, we might add, of the body, is developed and strengthened by use, and impaired by disuse. Exercise of even a weak imagination, if persistent and regular, will greatly tend to improve it. Of course Nature does more for some than for others, and it is not to be expected that each imagination will become the equal of every other, nor that all men will become geniuses in this respect more than in any other. Not every man will become a 'Samson in physical strength, however carefully he cultivates his body; but every healthy man may gain great additions to his strength, such as he would not have if he did not practise those exercises which imply muscular force and energy. The analogy holds with reference to the Imagination. The man who diligently uses such powers as he has, whether small or moderate, will find them developing into greater effectiveness.

Strengthened by use and impaired by disuse.

The Imagination is also cultivated by the **Study of the Ideal Creations** of great artists, poets, orators, and literary men. To see much of these, to become interested in and inspired by them, is to have enkindled in us a desire to imitate them, and to fill our minds with representations which can but powerfully influence our own characters. No one can be familiar with the works of Homer and Virgil and Shakespeare and Milton,

The study of ideal creations of great artists.

of Raphael and Michael Angelo, of Canova and Thorwald-sen, without catching something of the spirit that animated those great artists.

The **Study of Nature** is also an important means of culti-vating the Imagination. Most people, it is true, unless they are immured perpetually in cities, have access to Nature ; but there are comparatively few who are impressed with the marvellous beauties, the grandeur and sublimity, that are found almost everywhere by those who are disposed to look for them. The habit of observation is wanting in many, and even where it exists it is frequently directed to those par-ticulars which have nothing to do with our æs-thetic susceptibilities. The farmer, if he be an observant man at all, is likely to be thinking of the capa-bilities of the soil in relation to crops, grazing, etc. The civil engineer would be regarding the facilities for road-building, or for railways, looking out for water-powers and the construction of canals. So of many others who have particular interests in mind. But even some of these and many others could, by a little effort, direct their observation to such pictures of the aspect of Nature as would tend to excite, interest, and develop the Imagina-tion and the Taste.

Study of nature.

Beauties of nature, even when visible, frequently not observed.

It is to be remarked, that while the aspects of Nature are often beautiful in themselves, there is still greater beauty in what is suggested than in what actually ex-ists. Hence such scenes appeal to the idealizing power in the beholder. If this be wanting, it is not strange that the external aspect imparts no pleasure, and no sense of beauty. It is not a product of the Imagina-tion to present to the mind itself, or to describe or repre-

More beauty suggested than per-ceived.

sent to another, such a scene *just as it is.* The mind must add something of its own. A bare photograph is not a work either of Imagination or of Art. A man may imitate without idealizing, but it is only in the latter Suggestive that his Imagination comes into play. Take the illustration. following from Byron : —

> " She walks in beauty, like the night
>   Of cloudless climes and starry skies ;
> And all that's best of dark and bright
>   Meet in her aspect and her eyes :
> Thus mellowed to that tender light
>   Which heaven to gaudy day denies."

Here the poet wishes to describe a woman's beauty, one characteristic of which is that the dark and light so mingle, both in her general appearance and in her eyes, as to greatly enhance the effect of both. But instead of saying this in the commonplace way I have just indicated, he thinks of a night in a region where the atmosphere is pure, and the stars come out in full force, the very darkness rendering their light incalculably more beautiful. This furnishes an apt simile, by using which he not only the better expresses his thought, but charms and captivates the reader as no literal description could possibly do.

PART III.

THE ELABORATIVE FACULTY.

CHAPTER I.

THOUGHT AND THINKING.

WE have seen that cognitions are presented to the mind through Sensation and Perception, and by the Inner-Sense, and that these make us acquainted with *Previous presentations.* certain qualities, energies, and operations of the external world and of the mind itself, and that we class these all under the general term **Phenomena.** We have moreover seen that cognitions once in the mind are liable to re-present themselves under well-de-*All these cognitions are of individuals, not classes.* fined conditions as implied in the laws of Association, and that, while not directly subject to the control of the will, they are indirectly affected by it, so that we can within certain limits choose what subjects of contemplation shall be present in our minds; and that they there take the different forms of Fantasy, Memory, and Imagination. All these *Known as intuitive.* powers have for their objects the cognition of individuals, and not of groups or classes as such. The general name that has been given to the aggregate of these powers, including those of the Reason or regulative faculty, not yet considered, is **Intuitive Faculties.**

We come now to another set of faculties entirely different from those first considered, and which are known as the **Discursive** or **Elaborative Faculties.** These *The discursive or elaborative faculties.* furnish no new material to the mind, but they take the cognitions furnished by the other faculties and work them over into new forms which furnish additional knowledge. The processes and products of this

Thought and thinking.

faculty constitute what is called **Thinking** or **Thought.** In strict propriety Thinking is the process, and Thought the product, of the discursive faculties; but by many if not by most writers, Thought is used somewhat indiscriminately for both the operation and the result.

Thought has in the past been used very largely by writers, as comprehending all the operations of the intellect and as "co-extensive with consciousness." [1]

Thought now restricted to the discursive operations of the mind.

But by most of our best recent writers it is restricted to the processes and product of the discursive faculties. The phenomena of Thought are known under the general heads of Conception, Judgment, and Reasoning. These also imply certain minor and subsidiary powers and processes of which we shall become cognizant as we go on. These are usually all grouped together and called the **Logical** or **Rational** processes and faculties. For it is the department of mind here considered with which the study of Logic is concerned.

It is obvious that this is a higher department of man's intellectual nature than any of which we have heretofore taken notice. It is by thinking that we arrive

This a higher department of mind than any heretofore considered.

at the most important and the most difficult of the knowledge of which we can come into possession. "By Thought we know effects from their causes, and causes through their effects; we believe in powers whose actings we can only directly discern, and infer powers in objects which we have never tested nor observed; we explain what has happened by

[1] Sir William Hamilton.

referring it to laws of necessity or reason, and we pre-
dict what will happen by rightly interpreting what has
occurred. By thinking we rise to the unseen from that
which is seen, to the laws of Nature from the facts of
Nature, to the laws of spirit from the phenomena of spirit,
and to God from the universe of matter and of spirit,
whose powers reveal His energy, and whose ends and
adaptations manifest His thoughts and character." [1]

Let us take an instance exemplifying *what is meant by
thinking.* I look out of my window and see a tree. So
far as sense-perception goes, I cognize an object Illustrative
of a certain form and size and color or colors. instance.
I know that it is an external object and that it exists. So
far, and possibly further, I have done no perceptible thinking — possibly none at all. But I also know that there
are certain causes for the existence of the tree. I know
that it must have grown, though I have never seen it
grow. I know that it grew from a seed, and that seed was
in the fruit of another tree, which I have good reason to
think grew also from another seed, and so on in an indefinite series. But, coming back again to the present tree, I
compare it with several other trees that I have in my
mind, — hemlock, spruce, pine, oak, birch, maple, beech ; I
know that it is a maple; this from the shape of its leaves
and the character of the bark. I also know that it is likely
to be the parent of other trees, and that these trees will be
maples, and not oaks or pines ; and that from these will
come still other trees that will also be maples. I also
know that the wood of this tree is of a certain character;
that it will have a peculiar kind of utility for fuel; that it
can be made of a certain use as building material, or for

1 President Porter: The Human Intellect.

furniture, or for other purposes ; also, that when it is of a certain size, at a certain season of the year, from an incision sap will flow, from which can be manufactured sugar of a peculiar flavor and value. All these things, and many more, I know or believe, not from perception or the testimony of others, but by **Thinking**, — that is, by judging and reasoning.

CHAPTER II.

CONCEPTION AND CONCEPTS.

By many writers the term **Conception** is made to do the double duty of representing both the process and the product. But it seems to me that when we have two different things, and two words which may be applied to them respectively, and especially *Double mean ing of "con ception."* where this fact exists to any considerable extent, it is both a more desirable and more economical use of language to avail ourselves of this distinction. Accordingly I propose to use the word *conception* for the power or process of the mind, and *concept* for the product.

Conception, then, as a process, is divided into several distinct operations; namely, *analysis, abstraction, comparison,* and *generalization.* *Several dis tinct opera tions.*

Let us suppose that we perceive an object. We are sometimes taught that our perception is of an object immediately and instantly. Doubtless in a certain sense this is true. Long before we have come to observe our mental operations we have formed *Not always conscious of the processes of cognition.* habits of rapid perception, that is, of so quickly uniting our perceptions of different parts that we cease to pay attention to the various minute steps of the process, or even to be aware that there is any process at all. Thus, apparently, on seeing a house, a tree, a horse, a rose, or an orange, we instantly cognize the aggregate individual in each case, and do not cognize noticeably the several qual-

ities which we have swiftly united in our minds to form
Still there is the object. Nevertheless there is a process, a
a process. perception, first of the different parts or elements, and then a synthesis of these into a whole. This is
evident from the fact that often when we see a new object,
and especially if it be a somewhat though perhaps only
moderately complicated object, we spend some time in
considering the separate parts and their relations to each
other, before we can be said to have any definite perception
of the individual whole. This is the case even when we
see objects with which we are more or less familiar, in a
dim light or under unfavorable circumstances. As we say,
sometimes, "I cannot quite make it out;" and it is only
by more carefully noting the parts or qualities and their
relations, that the familiar object finally re-forms itself in
our minds.

Still under the habits of perception which we have formed,
we do so instantly take in the object perceived that there
is not the least apparent synthesis of parts and qualities.
Hence to all practical intents we perceive the whole before
The first con- we perceive its parts. Consequently the first
scious pro- operation of which we are conscious in the process that of
analysis. cess of conception is that of **Analysis**. We
separate the object into its parts.

Let us take a concrete case. I see before me an object
which has a certain effect on the eye, — that is, it is of a
certain hue. It has, as I note, a certain form and size.
I touch it, and it is soft and smooth and yielding, but not
fluid. It has also a certain odor of which I readily become
aware. There are a dozen other qualities which it might
be difficult to specify, but which the observer knows. Now
I may do either of two things: I may abstract a single

quality, or several of the qualities, and proceed from the former or the latter, according to the object I have in view. Let us take the single quality which first affects me through the eye. I make this color the sole object of my attention, leaving out all the other qualities. This is **Abstraction** — a *drawing away from* all the others for the sake of exclusive consideration. This is the second step in the process.

Abstraction.

The third step is that of **Comparison**. Having fixed upon the color of the object, I look about me at the multitude of objects on every side. I compare their various qualities with this particular one, which I have in mind. Some of these qualities appeal to the ear, and others to the touch, and others to other senses, and thus are entirely unlike this. But I see several qualities which, like this, appeal directly to the eye, and yet they differ from one another. They are alike in some respects, but diverse in others. But among these various colors I find several instances of substantial similarity to this. I decide that these are alike. So far Comparison.

Comparison.

I now proceed to put all those objects having this quality which I have found in a large number of instances, into a group or class by themselves. Wherever I find anything which is thus characterized, a flower, a bit of ribbon, the plumage of a bird, the clouds at sunset, a lady's dress, a burning coal, etc.,— these are all put into a class by themselves. This is **Generalization**,—an identification of the quality in any number of different objects.

Classification or generalization.

It only remains to give a name to this class. For, though the process of Conception is complete at the point at which we have arrived, in order to assure its utility and availability, it must have a name. So

Denomination.

this is added to the process by many writers, and called **Denomination**. The name that we give to this class which we have formed, and which, when we have gathered up

We call the whole class thus formed a concept. under one name, we call a **Concept**, is that of *red things*. Every object that has this quality we call a *red thing*, though we ordinarily use the designating adjective with some noun, and say, a red rose, a red ribbon, etc. This we may do, or we may carry our observation further, and keep the color separate from all its substances, and give it a name by itself, calling it *redness*. In this case we have an abstract, instead of a concrete Concept.

There is a *second method* of Conception. We take an object which is presented to our senses. We observe, as

Another method of conception. before, its particular qualities, making an Analysis of it. We take particular note of several of these qualities, which we abstract from the others; among these, that it is an *animal* (which must previously, of course, have been generalized), that it has a bushy tail and mane, an arching neck, a peculiarly shaped head, and four feet. We compare this with other animals, and among them, while we find a great multitude that have certain of these characteristics, there is a smaller number, the individuals of which have all of them. These we put

Conception of a horse. together in a class, and call them *horses*. Now *horse* becomes the name of the class — it is a *term* or **Concept**, and it is given to a class, and so desig-

A class every individual in which may be called a horse. nates the class that every member of it may be called by this name — *a horse* — every member also having all the qualities to which I first referred. Or we might have taken the single quality of this object, namely, its having four feet, and, using this quality as a test, and putting all animals having it in a class, have given this class the name *quadruped.*

We are now prepared to give the complete definition of the Concept. It is " *that product of the mind* Definition of *which results from Generalization whereby many* concept. *individuals are combined in one class, through one or more similar qualities, and are indicated by a common term."* [1]

Thus we have classes numbering hundreds and thousands of individuals, all individuals in each called by a common name, as horse, dog, man, tree, house, etc. Each horse is different from every other horse, though every horse has certain qualities that belong to all horses, and every individual horse, whatever peculiarities he may have, has in any case these qualities and may therefore be designated by this term.

HIGHER AND LOWER CONCEPTS.

Concepts may be formed, not only from individuals, but from other concepts or classes. That is, there Concepts are *classes of classes.* This gives rise to the idea formed from of higher and lower concepts. These higher cepts. concepts are formed from the lower in the same way that the lower are formed from the individuals. The following diagram will illustrate what is meant by this.

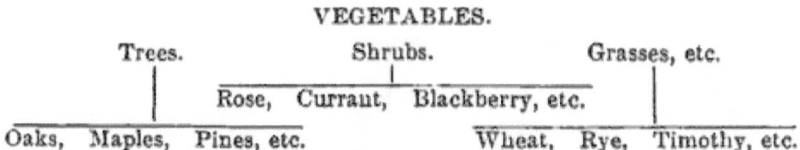

VEGETABLES.

Trees.　　　　Shrubs.　　　Grasses, etc.

Rose, Currant, Blackberry, etc.

Oaks, Maples, Pines, etc.　　Wheat, Rye, Timothy, etc.

This might be extended still further. Here we have, for instance, an oak. On examining it we find that it has

[1] Atwater's Logic.

certain qualities in common with maples, pines, etc.   Now oaks, pines, and maples are themselves concepts, having under them respectively several lower concepts, these being generalized from individuals.   But attention is principally called to this fact, that the concepts named have certain qualities in common, and these qualities taken together constitute the qualities of *trees*.   This, then, becomes a higher concept generalized from the concepts oaks, maples, pines.   Hence every oak, as also every pine, and every one of several other concepts, is a *tree*.

Still higher concepts. We may carry the generalization still higher. Thus, trees when compared with shrubs, grasses, and some other concepts, will be found to have certain qualities which are also common to all of them. These we combine together under one term and call them *vegetables*.   Every tree is a vegetable, every shrub and every kind of grass is a vegetable.   Of course, as the higher contains all the lower, it must necessarily contain all that they contain.   Hence all classes of trees and all classes of shrubs and grasses, and all individuals of each class, are also vegetables.

There is another noticeable feature in the relation of **Denomination of objects corresponds with increase of qualities, and vice versa.** these higher and lower concepts as presented in the diagram.   Perhaps if we put it in a single column we may be able to comprehend it more clearly.   Thus : —

> Vegetable.
>
> Tree.
>
> Maple.
>
> Sugar Maple.
>
> This Sugar Maple.

As we go from below upward we notice that the *number of objects* in the several classes or concepts increases. Thus, at the bottom we have only a single individual — one sugar maple. In the next above we have this particular sugar maple and many others. In the class above this we have not only this sugar maple and all other sugar maples, but all other kinds of maples besides. In the next higher class are comprised all those of which we have spoken — all the maples and the classes and individuals included in them — also all oaks and pines and elms, and all other trees of every sort. While in the highest class are contained all the trees, and in addition to these, all shrubs and grasses and whatever else comes under the head of vegetables. There are very many more vegetables than there are trees ; many more trees than maples; and many individual sugar maples.

As we go from the individual to the summum genus the number of objects increases.

On the other hand we shall find a diminution as well as an increase as we go from the lower to the higher ; but the diminution will be in the number of *qualities*, and not of *objects*. *This sugar maple* has all the qualities that belong to all sugar maples, and some that no other sugar maple has. Sugar maples also have all the qualities that maples as such have, and some which they do not have, and which make these not only maples, but sugar maples. Again, maples have all the qualities that belong to trees, and others that are not implied in the concept tree. So of trees in relation to vegetables. In every upward step from lower to higher concepts, there is a dropping off of qualities and a taking on of objects. This phenomenon may be repre-

But there is a diminution of the number of qualities.

sented in two columns, the one increasing as we go from the top to the bottom, and the other decreasing: —

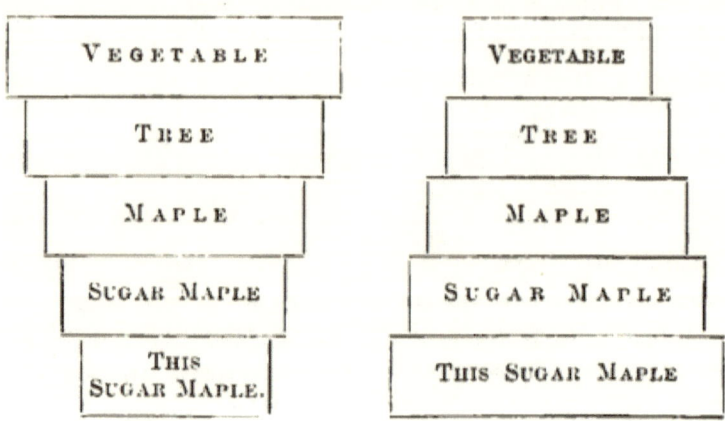

Here, then, we have two wholes; the one of **Extension**, the other of **Intension**. The former has reference to the *quantity* of the concept, or the number of objects contained under it. The latter pertains to the *quality* of the concept: that is, the number of different characteristics implied in it. It has been observed that as we go up the column, the number of objects increases and the number of qualities diminishes; or the extension increases as the intension diminishes. As we go down the column, the intension increases and the extension diminishes. In other words, the extension and intension are in the inverse proportion to each other.

The two wholes of extension and intension.

The highest class of the objects under consideration is called the **Summum Genus**. The lowest class, that cannot be further divided, except into individuals, is called the **Infima Species**. The *individual*, as its name implies, is that which is *not logically divisible*.

Summum genus and infima species.

It may be physically divided into parts, but these parts would have no logical concept of which the individual was a member. Thus we may divide animals into vertebrates, radiates, mollusks, etc.; vertebrates into quadrupeds and bipeds; quadrupeds into horses, dogs, goats, sheep, etc.; horses into Shetland ponies, mustangs, war-horses, and others; war-horses into individuals, of which Bucephalus may be one. Now Bucephalus may be killed and divided up into head, legs, hide, entrails, and carcass; but none of these is a horse: whereas in the divisions previous to this, each part or division in all the grades may be called by the name of the class above it. Bucephalus is a war-horse; a war-horse is a horse, and a horse is a quadruped, and a quadruped is a vertebrate, and a vertebrate is an animal, as is each of the subordinate classes through all the grades down to the individual Bucephalus. The *Absolute Summum Genus* is the highest possible class, that which can never be a species. Thus Being cannot be a species of anything; it includes all objects in the universe under it, and has but a single quality.

The individual not logically divisible.

In physical divisions no part can be called by the name of the whole.

Absolute summum genus.

It is of great importance to have accurate conceptions. There can be no healthy and valuable thinking without this. The three great virtues of thinking are **Clearness, Distinctness,** and **Adequacy.** The three corresponding vices are **Confusion, Obscurity,** and **Inadequacy.**

The three great virtues of conception.

A conception is *clear* when we can separate a particular concept from all others. It is somewhat the same as in perception. We clearly perceive a man when we distinguish him from other objects. In the dimness of the

Clearness. light or in the distance we may not be able to make out clearly whether the object seen is a stump, or a bush, or some animal; but as we come nearer, or the light grows stronger, we satisfy ourselves that it is a man, and not one of the other objects mentioned. What is true of perception is true of other cognitions and especially of concepts. Many persons do not clearly distinguish Zoölogy from Natural History, Percept from Perception, Thought from Mental Activity, Trade from Commerce, Pride from Vanity, Self-respect from Pride, or Selfishness from Self-love. Yet clearness in thinking demands this discrimination, and for want of this discrimination arises the vice of mental confusion.

Distinctness of conception exists not only when we are able to separate the cognition from other cognitions, but

Distinctness. also to designate the marks which distinguish it. There are many cases where we have what is called a clear cognition, but at the same time it is not distinct. In the illustration previously given, of knowing that the object was a man, and not a stump or a bush, most persons might make the discrimination that would enable them to decide positively that the object was a man: but the great majority, if asked for their reasons for so deciding, could not give them — in other words, they cannot give the *marks* of the object. This is often the case in all sorts of cognitions. Thus in the familiar illustration of the handwriting of intimate friends. We see a letter or other document in a certain style of chirography, and we at once decide that it is the handwriting of a certain person with whose style of writing we are familiar. We have no doubt about it, and on the witness-stand in a court-room under oath, might feel no hesitation in asserting this. But if the cross-examining lawyer should ask us *how we know* that this is the handwriting of the person alleged, we probably should not be able to answer. We could not give the marks that distinguish it from the writing of other persons. So, too, we meet persons whom we know instantly. They are not very unlike a score of other persons whom we know; but if asked to identify them by particular marks, we could not do so; we could not tell in what respect any one of them differed from any one of a certain number of other persons. An expert in penmanship, in the case of handwriting, could do this; so could a man who had made a study of physiognomies, point out the particular marks which distinguish one man from another. To be able to do this is to have a distinct cognition. It is so in the use of common terms. The man who has only a clear conception will be accurate enough for most purposes; but there are times when greater precision is required, and then distinctness of conception is necessary.

It is frequently necessary to go even further than this. Our conceptions must in certain cases not only be clear and distinct, but they must be **Adequate**. We Adequate- must be able to separate the concept from other ness. concepts, and to give the marks by which this separate concept may be tested; we must be able also to analyze the marks themselves and give their The marks of elements; in other words, to give the *marks* the marks. *of the marks.* Thus in the concept man: I know that he differs from other objects; I can also give the marks by which he is thus distinguished, — as, that he is ani-

mal and rational. If asked to explain what I mean by
these terms, I must be able to give the marks of animal
and rational, and show that the former is distinguished
by organization and sentiency; and the latter by intelligence and reason. Careful, exact, and critical thought
must have all these virtues.

DIVISION AND DEFINITION.

These virtues of which I have spoken as essential to all
good thinking will be very greatly promoted by the care-
Office of
division.   ful study of the **Division** and **Definition** of concepts. The former of these terms relates to the
explication of the concept considered as a whole of *exten-*
Office of
definition.   *sion;* that is, with reference to the quantity, or
the number, of objects comprised under it.
Definition, on the other hand, relates to the quality of the
concept: that is, it is the unfolding of the whole of *inten-*
sion. This, then, is to be particularly borne in mind: that
the division of a concept consists in separating it into its
constituent parts; and that definition consists in separating
it into its constituent qualities.

RULES FOR DIVISION.

1. It *must proceed from genera to species* in regular order
and not arbitrarily. To divide men into Europeans, In-
Must pro-
ceed from
genera to
species.   dians, Australians, Chinamen, Mexicans, and
Malaysians, would be a violation of this rule.
They might be divided geographically, first,
according to continental arrangement, and then each of
these chief divisions might be subdivided.

2. There *must be one fundamental principle* of division.

It would not do, for instance, to divide Americans into Virginians, New Englanders, Protestants, Catholics, Agriculturists, Clergymen, etc. Some might thus be found in two or three divisions, and some might not be included anywhere.

One fundamental principle.

3. The divisions *must be mutually exclusive;* otherwise we might be involved in the same errors as noticed under Rule 2.

Mutually exclusive.

4. The *sum of all the parts should be exactly equal to the concept to be divided;* each member must be less than the division or class to be divided.

Sum of the parts exactly equal to the whole.

5. It *must not be by negatives,* or what is called in Logic by Infinitation. To divide men into Englishmen and those who are not Englishmen, is a complete division, but it is also of no value.

Not by negatives.

I have already spoken of the difference between logical division and physical division. The individual cannot be logically divided, for the reason that its several parts have no logical relation to the concepts of which it is a member. No one of the parts of a horse can be called a horse. But each individual horse is a quadruped, a mammal, a vertebrate, an animal.

Logical and physical division.

It will be readily noticed that this subject of division is one of great importance in all our thinking, and does not confine itself exclusively to scientific classification. It is most essential to a man who is called upon for public addresses, in the writing of essays and treatises, in plans of business and of statesmanship. One can hardly set forth clearly any purpose or project without some practical acquaintance with these principles.

Importance of division.

RULES FOR DEFINITION.

Definition gives the marks of conceptions, and thus bounds them off from all other conceptions, so that we not only know that they differ, but in what respect they differ.

Import of definition.

1. Definition *must be by marks which distinguish the thing defined* from all the other members of the next class above it. In other words, it must be by *essential marks*. By essential marks we mean that the definition must be in terms of the class above the concept to be defined, and those qualities which distinguish it from other concepts of the same class. The concept to be defined is always a species of some genus, and it must be defined in terms of that genus and the *differentia*, or the marks by which it differs from that genus. The formula may be expressed thus: Species = Genus + Differentia. As an illustrative example, take the following: —

By essential marks.

Man = Animal + Rational; or

Man is a rational animal. Here we have *Man*, the concept to be defined; and the definition, consisting of *Animal*, the genus of Man, with the addition of the differentia *Rational*, which marks him off from animals generally.

2. A definition *should never include the name of the thing defined,* or any term etymologically connected with it. Thus, we should not define *vivacity* as "speaking or writing in a vivacious manner." This is tautological. It also is similar to defining in a circle, which is to be avoided. Thus it would not be logical to define light as "an illuminating force," and then, if asked to explain further, to define *illuminating* as "the giving of light."

Should never include the name of the definitum.

3. It *must include all the objects covered by the concept* to be defined, and nothing else. If we define a *horse* as a *quadruped*, we are including something more than the thing to be defined. If we define it as a *Shetland pony*, we are not including enough, since there are other horses besides Shetland ponies.

Must include all the objects to be defined, and nothing else.

4. It *must not be by negatives;* as, to define a *sheep* as *not a goat*, gives us no positive information whatever.

Must not be by negatives.

5. It *must be precise, and free from surplus words.* " Parallel lines are those that never meet," is not an adequate definition, since they might be in different planes and never meet, and yet not be parallel. " Parallelograms are rectilineal, four-sided figures, whose opposite sides are parallel and equal," is not a good definition, since the words " and equal " are unnecessary, and they are therefore misleading, as giving the impression that there may be parallelograms whose opposite sides are parallel but not equal.

Free from surplus words.

CHAPTER III.

JUDGMENT.

Judgment *is that act of the mind by which, on the comparison of two concepts, or an individual and a concept,*
Definition.   *we affirm that they agree or disagree.* Thus
we take *bird* and *animal.* On comparing them
together, if we fully understand these concepts, we find
that *bird* has all the qualities that belong to *animal;* we
may therefore assert that they agree; that is, that a bird
is an animal. So, on the other hand, if we compare the
conceptions *man* and *angel,* we shall find that neither of
them has the qualities that belong to the other; hence we
may assert that they do not agree, or that no man is an
angel.

Judgment, it will be observed, is a mental process. A
judgment is a mental product; and when expressed in
A judgment   language the expression is called a *proposition.*
and a proposi-   It always consists of two *terms* (from *termini,*
tion.   the extremes) and a *copula.* One of the terms
is called the **Subject,** and the other the **Predicate.** The
Predicate   subject is that of which something is asserted.
and subject.   The predicate is that which is asserted of the
subject. The copula is that by which the assertion is
made, and is always some form of the present indicative
of the verb *to be,* or is capable of being reduced to that
form. Thus, in the proposition, " Cæsar conquered Gaul,"

there is expressed no form of the verb *to be*, and there is no copula separate from the predicate. But what is implied, and will fully appear when the proposition is fully explicated, is, "Cæsar is the man who conquered Gaul."

The following analysis of the process of judgment has been given by Crousaz, as quoted by Sir William Hamilton: "In fine, when we judge, we must have, Crousaz' analysis of a judgment. in the first place, at least two notions; in the second place, we compare these; in the third, we recognize that one contains or excludes the other; and in the fourth, we acquiesce in the recognition."

Judgments are variously classified, according to the points of view from which they are contemplated. First, they are regarded in respect to **Quantity**. By Judgments classified. the quantity of a judgment is meant *the relation of the predicate to the extension of the subject;* that is, whether the predicate is of the whole or some Quantity. indefinite part of the subject. With respect to Quantity, judgments are either **Universal**, **Particular**, or **Singular**. They are universal when the predicate is affirmed or denied of the subject taken dis- Universal. tributively, or when the assertion is concerning the whole of the subject, as, "All men are mortal;" "No horses are bipeds." Judgments are particular when the predicate is affirmed or denied of an indefinite Particular. part of the subject, as, "Some men are poets;" "Some animals are vertebrates." Judgments are singular when the predicate is affirmed or denied of an individual, as, "Columbus discovered America;" Singular. or of a plurality of individuals taken collectively, as, "This army is invincible." Singular judgments are treated as universals, since the predication is of the **Singular judgments treated as universals.** whole subject. Also, when any definite part of a subject is taken, the judgment is to be regarded as universal. "These men are natives of Ireland." Here the predication is of all that is contained in the subject, and the word with its limiting adjunct is a definite whole as it would not be if we were **Distributed terms.** to say "some men." A word is said to be Distributed when the whole of the concept is taken; it is Undistributed when only an indefinite part is taken. The **Quality** of a judgment has reference to the **Quality, affirmative or negative.** agreement or disagreement of the subject and predicate. The distinction of judgments in this respect is that they are either Affirmative or Negative. Propositions are affirmative when they have an affirmative copula, and negative when the copula is negative. Sometimes the proposition is affirmative when it may seem to be negative, and *vice versa.* "All men who are not righteous are wicked," is an affirmative proposition, since the negative falls not in the copula, but modifies the subject. So, too, "Few men are saints," is in form affirmative, but virtually negative, because it is equivalent to saying that "Most men are not saints."

In respect to **Quantity** and **Quality**, then, there are, according **Four kinds of judgments.** ing to the old logicians, four kinds of judgments, which it is customary to symbolize by the letters A, E, I, and O, thus :

Universal Affirmative,	A.
Universal Negative,	E.
Particular Affirmative,	I.
Particular Negative,	O.

The later logicians have added two more kinds based upon the doctrine of a Quantified or Distributed Predicate. According to the ordinary forms of affirm- Distributed ative propositions, the predicate is not distrib- predicate. uted; that is, there is nothing in the form that indicates its distribution. Still it may be actually distributed from the very nature of the case. Thus, when we say, "All men are mortal," we know that all men are not all the mortals there are. So, too, when we say, "Men are rational animals," so far as the form of the proposition is concerned there may be other rational animals besides men. But as a matter of fact, we know that the two terms "men" and "rational animals" are co-extensive, since men are all the rational animals there are; therefore the predicate is distributed as well as the subject. So, too, when we say, "Some quadrupeds are horses," they are *all* the horses; hence, in fact though not in form, the predicate is distributed. We thus have two more kinds of judgments which are of some value in logic. They are called

Universal Substitutive, U.

Particular Substitutive, Y.

But these we need not discuss further.

Judgments are further divided into **Categorical** and **Hypothetical**. A Categorical judgment is one in which one concept is directly affirmed or denied of Categorical another, or of an individual. A Hypothetical judgments. judgment is one in which the assertion is contingent, or depends upon some other fact or statement. Hy- Hypothetical pothetical judgments are divided into **Conditional**, judgments. **Disjunctive**, and **Dilemmatic**. A Conditional judgment is

one in which such a relation exists between two **members** of the judgment, known respectively as Antecedent
Conditional   and Consequent, that if the former is true,
judgments.   the latter is true also ; and if the latter is false,
the former is also false ; but if the former is false, or the
latter true, nothing follows as to the other; as, " If A is
B, C is D."

A Disjunctive judgment asserts the connection between
the subject and predicate with an alternative indicated by
Disjunctive   the particles *either* and *or*, as " John will either
judgments.   eat his cake or keep it." If one is denied, the
other is true. A Dilemmatic judgment involves a combination of the Conditional and Disjunctive. Thus, " If we
Dilemmatic   say John's baptism was from heaven, we con-
judgments.   demn ourselves ; if we say it was from men,
the people will stone us." That is, " If we either say it
was from heaven, or of men, we shall either condemn ourselves, or the people will stone us."

Judgments are either **Problematical** or **Assertory** or
Apodictic. They are Problematical when we are neither
Problematic   certain of them ourselves, nor can we make
judgments.   others certain of them : as the judgment that
" Jupiter is inhabited." Such statements can be only
matters of opinion. An Assertory judgment is one which
Assertory   may be subjectively certain, but not objectively
judgments.   so ; that is, the asserter may be certain of it,
but cannot make any one else certain of it. For instance,
I am certain of some mental affection or operation ; but I
cannot prove this to another, only so far as he takes my
Apodictic   word for it. Such are matters of religious
judgments.   faith. Apodictic judgments are those which
are both subjectively and objectively certain ; they are

known beyond any peradventure to the person who asserts them, and they compel the assent of all who hear them. The statements that a part of a thing is less than the whole, that the sum of all the parts is equal to the whole, that two things equal to a third thing are equal to each other, are of this kind. All necessary truths come under this head.

Judgment is the essential and radical factor in all thinking or thought; and thinking or thought is the process or product of the discursive faculties. In *Judgment* a rudimentary and primitive way judgment is *the essential factor in all* involved in all the operations of this depart- *thought.* ment of the mind. Its conspicuous characteristic is comparison, and this operation we found almost in the very beginning of the process of generalization, or the forming of concepts. So that, though in its logical sense and use of the judgment, it must have a concept for *Judgment* one of its terms, yet in its strictly psychologi- *preceding* cal character it must have existed in each mind *conception.* before concepts could be formed. Still this process in its rudimentary character is so subtile, evanescent, and vague, that little notice is taken of it, and the statements concerning it are, for the most part, unsatisfactory. Nevertheless it must not be ignored, or lost sight of, that all real thinking is essentially judging. Judgment *All real* is the prominent element in all reasoning, *thinking is essentially* not only as a condition for this process but as *judging.* being a part of it. We always reason in judgments, starting from judgments, which in the syllogism are compared with each other, judging of the truth of the conclusion, which is also itself a judgment.

This thinking or judging, too, is, so far as we can discern, a perpetual operation of the mind. It is doubtful if there is any action of the intellect from which it is absent; or any portion of our waking or possibly of our sleeping hours when it ceases. If a person should take himself up at almost any moment, and inquire concerning the present or immediately past operation of his mind, if he recalls it at all, it is exceedingly probable that he has been comparing certain thoughts or concepts or representations, and affirming or denying something concerning their agreement. His mind has been asserting that this is this, or that it is not something else. The objects may be those of perception or of memory or reflection, but there always accompanies the mental act some thought or judgment.

"All thought is a comparison, a recognition of similarity or difference, a conjunction or disjunction; in other words, a synthesis or analysis of its objects. In conception, that is, in the formation of concepts (or general notions), it compares, disjoins or conjoins attributes; in an act of judgment, it compares, disjoins, or conjoins concepts; in reasoning it compares, disjoins, or conjoins judgments. In each step of this process there is one essential element; to think, to compare, or disjoin, it is necessary to recognize one thing through or under another. It is in performing this act of thinking a thing under a general notion, that we are said to understand or comprehend it. For example: An object is presented, say, a book; this object determines an impression, and I am even conscious of the impression, but without recognizing to myself what the thing is; in that case there is only a perception, and not properly a thought. But, suppose I do recognize it for what it is, compare it with or reduce it under a certain concept, class, or comple-

Sir William Hamilton on the functions of judgment.

ment of attributes, which I call *book*; in that case there is more than a perception — there is a thought." [1] This will help us to understand what is meant when we say that rudimentary or primitive judgment is involved in all our discursive processes.

[1] Sir William Hamilton: Lectures on Logic.

CHAPTER IV.

REASONING AND INFERENCE.

WHAT is meant by **Reasoning** is the deriving from judgments previously given, of other judgments founded

Definition.

upon them; or "that operation of the mind through which it forms one judgment from many others." The constitution of things is such that certain facts are so connected with certain other facts, or

Existence of certain things implied in that of others.

so involved in them, that the existence of the former implies that of the latter, and if we know the one we know the other also, though we may have no means of knowing the latter, except through the medium of our knowledge of the former. Thus, if I see a man on this side of a long river at ten o'clock in the morning, and see him on the other side at eleven o'clock, I know that he has crossed the river in the meantime, though I have not seen him do so, nor in any way perceived the act of crossing, nor have learned it through any testimony. I know it simply from the relations of the other known facts, which are such that if they are or were actual, this must also be actual. And I know this just as certainly as if I had myself perceived it. This I take to be substantially a type of most of our reasoning.

The determination of the relation of facts, whether perceptions, acts, deliverances of the Inner-Sense, or of the regulative faculty, is by a process of the mind which has already been described, and which is designated as **Judgment**. The expression of this in language is called a **Proposition**. As previously shown, the essential element in reasoning, as in all preliminary thinking processes, is judgment. We reason from judgment to judgments; and the determining of the relations of judgments, and what is involved in them, and whether it be inferential or not, is of the nature of a judgment.

Reasoning is commonly divided into **Deductive** and **Inductive** — or reasoning from general classes to particular classes or to individuals, and reasoning from individuals or particular classes to general facts and principles. <small>Deductive and inductive.</small>

A difference is also to be observed between **Reasoning** and **Inference**. The difference is much the same as between **Analytic** and **Synthetic** reasoning. In the former case the conclusion is stated first in the form of a proposition to be proved; in the latter the grounds or facts from which we reason are stated first, and the conclusion inferred from them. <small>Reasoning and inference.</small>

All oaks are vegetables, because all trees are vegetables, and all oaks are trees.

This is analytic reasoning; that is, a proposition is stated, and we look about for its proof. We separate into parts, and compare the several parts with another object in such a way that we find a substantial reason for the truth of the proposition. <small>Analytic reasoning.</small>

> All trees are vegetables;
> All oaks are trees;
> All oaks are vegetables.

This is synthetic. Two propositions are found in such relations to each other that they necessarily imply a third, *Synthetic reasoning.* or by a combination — a synthesis of the elements of the two — we have a third which is an inference from them.

Inference mediate and immediate. Inference is further either **Immediate** or **Mediate**. It is immediate when one judgment is inferred from another without the intervention or mediation of a third judgment. There are several forms of *Opposition.* Immediate Inference, the most common of which are by **Opposition** and by **Conversion**.

OPPOSITION.

Two judgments are said to be in opposition *when they have the same subject and predicate, but differ in quantity or quality, or both.* When they differ in quality only, it is called *Contrary* or *Sub-contrary* opposition.

When they differ in quantity only, it is called *Subaltern* opposition.

When they differ in both quality and quantity it is called *Contradictory* opposition.

The value of this method of reasoning is that we immediately infer from one proposition the truth or falsehood of the opposite.

All men are poets. A.

No men are poets. E.

These two propositions are in contrary opposition. From the truth of the former we infer the falsity of the latter; *Contrary opposition.* but not the truth of the latter from the falsity of the former; since both cannot be true, but both may be false, as in this particular case.

> Some men are poets.   I.
> Some men are not poets. O.

These are Sub-contraries. From the falsity of the one we infer the truth of the other; but from the <sub-contrary> truth of the one we infer nothing concerning <opposition.> the other, since they may both be true, as in this instance they are.

> All men are poets.   A.
> Some men are poets.   I.

and

> No men are poets.   E.
> Some men are not poets. O.

In each case if the former is true, the latter must be true also; but from the truth of the latter nothing follows concerning the former. From the falsehood of <subaltern> the latter the falsehood of the former follows; <opposition.> though from the falsehood of the former nothing follows concerning the latter.

> All men are poets.   A.
> Some men are not poets. O.
>
> No men are poets.   E.
> Some men are poets.   I.

Here it will be seen that in each case, if either of the two opposites be true, the other must be false; if either be false, the other must be true; and that one *must* <contradictory opposition.> be false and the other true. This is the strongest kind of opposition. This kind of inference is useful in cases where, though it would not be convenient, perhaps not possible, to prove the truth or falsehood of a particular proposition. we may nevertheless easily prove Value of in-
ference by
means of
opposition. the truth or falsehood of its opposite; and if the opposition is of the kind that serves our purpose, we may draw an immediate inference from the proposition proved as to the truth or falsehood of its opposite. Thus in any argument we say sometimes, "It is impossible to prove a negative." This is not always true, but it is sometimes true. In such a case as this, if we can find means to prove the truth of the contradictory of the proposition we wish to negative, this is equivalent to disproving the proposition in question, since the truth of the contradictory implies the falsehood of its opposite.

CONVERSION.

By this we mean the changing of places of the subject and predicate, in such a way that the *Converse* is an infer- Conversion
defined. ence from the *Convertend*. This is the only kind of illative conversion, or that in which an inference may be drawn from the original proposition to its converse. Thus, —

> Some men are wise beings;
> Some wise beings are men, —

is an illative conversion, since the latter proposition is a necessary and obvious inference from the former.

> All dogs are animals;
> All animals are dogs, —

this is conversion, but it is not illative; there is no inference of the latter from the former.

The general rule governing the logical character of conversion is that *no term must be distributed* Rule for *in the converse which was not distributed in* conversion. *the convertend.*

Conversion, in order to be logical, then, sometimes requires a change in quantity or quality. Hence the following different kinds of conversion.

1. **Simple Conversion** is when there is no change Simple either in quantity or quality, as, — conversion.

> Some Orientals are Christians;
> Some Christians are Orientals.
>
> No men are angels;
> No angels are men.

2. *Conversion by limitation*, or *per accidens*, as it is sometimes called, is when the quantity is changed Conversion from universal to particular. by limitation.

> All Germans are Europeans;
> All Europeans are Germans.

Here we could not make the inference by simple conversion that all Europeans are Germans. In no case are we warranted by the *form* of the conversion to infer a universal affirmative from a universal affirmative, or A from A. But there are cases in which we know more than Certain cases the form of the proposition implies, or know that where the predicate, the predicate, though not distributed in form, is though not in form dis- distributed in fact; as in the proposition, "All tributed, is men are rational animals." Here we know that so in fact. men are all the rational animals there are, though the *form* indicates nothing of the kind. Hence we are justified in saying that "All rational animals are men." But ordinarily we can convert A only by limitation.

3. *Conversion by negation* or contra-position is when the quality is changed. This is a somewhat awkward process, but nevertheless violates no law of thought. Take, for instance, the proposition, —

By negation.

> Some men are not poets.

We cannot infer from this that some poets are not men, but we can change the quality without changing the sense.

> Some men are non-poets ; or
>
> Some men are persons who are not poets.

That is, we transfer the negative particle from the copula to the predicate, and thus make an affirmative proposition of what was before a negative. We may now convert simply, —

> Some persons who are not poets are men ; or
>
> Some non-poets are men.

This method of inference by Conversion, like that by Opposition, is useful in many instances where it might not be convenient, or perhaps possible, to prove a certain proposition, but where we might easily prove its converse, and, this being proved, we can easily infer the needed judgment.

Utility of inference by conversion.

MEDIATE INFERENCE.

Three judgments involved, but to have some relation to each other.

As previously indicated, most of our reasoning involves three judgments. These are not *any* judgments selected at random or arbitrarily. Thus, if we say, —

> An army is a military organization;
> Washington was a patriot, —

we can infer nothing, since they have no such relation to each other as to imply a third. But when we say, —

> All horses are vertebrates;
> All Shetland ponies are horses;
> ∴ All Shetland ponies are vertebrates, —

we see at a glance that the relations of the first two propositions are such that the last inevitably follows.

Also, if we should say, —

> No men are angels;
> All Americans are men;
> ∴ No Americans are angels, —

we should be compelled to acknowledge that if the first two propositions are true, the last must be true also.

Mediate Reasoning is a process of the mind. When expressed in language it is called an **Argument**. An argument in regular form is a **Syllogism**. The syllogism consists of two parts; namely, that from which the proof proceeds, and that which is proved. *Reasoning, argument, and syllogism.* The former consists of two propositions called **Premises**. The latter is the **Conclusion**. The premises are *Major* and *Minor*. *Premises and conclusions.*

There are in every syllogism three terms, and only three: the *Major Term*, the *Minor Term*, and the *Middle Term*. The major term is the predicate of the conclusion, and the minor term the subject of the conclusion. The middle term is not found in the con- *Major, minor, and middle terms.*

clusion, but is found in both the premises. The major

Major and
minor prem-
ises.
premise is that proposition in which the major term is compared with the middle term; and the minor premise, that in which the minor term is compared with the middle term. The middle term, as

Function of
the middle
term.
will readily be seen, is the medium through which the relationship between the major and minor terms is established. Thus, in the case previously given, if some one should hear of oaks for the first time, but did not know what they were, and whether they were vegetables or not, but should be informed that they were trees, and knowing that trees were vegetables, it would be seen at once that, taking these two facts together, they imply a third; namely, that oaks are vegetables. This is brought about by the mediation of the middle term *trees.*

The great general principle of syllogistic reasoning is Aristotle's dictum, that " Whatever is affirmed or denied

Dictum of
Aristotle.
of any class taken distributively can be affirmed or denied of every class and every individual contained in that class." Sir William Hamilton, also, has

Hamilton's
maxim.
a maxim of general application to the effect that " Whatever may be affirmed or denied of a whole may be affirmed or denied of each of its parts." Dr. Hop-

Dr. Hopkins's
objection.
kins does not accept these as applicable to all kinds of syllogisms, or to all kinds of propositions from which inferences may be drawn. It is probable that, so far as the strict form is concerned, he is correct. Certainly it is not precisely on either of these principles that we proceed in the following deduction:

A is equal to B ;

C is equal to A ;

∴ C is equal to B, —

but rather on the mathematical axiom that things equal to a third thing are equal to each other. A certainly is not in this case a part of B, nor is it contained in it, except by a rather strained construction of language. The same is true of C in relation to A. Still instances of this kind are so rare that they may be regarded as exceptional, and the dictum and maxim hold good generally.

But we are to take note that reasoning is by no means generally so simple as this. An important question can seldom be settled by a single syllogism, nor by two, nor by half a dozen; frequently not by a score of syllogisms. Many pages, and sometimes whole volumes, have to be written to prove a single proposition. A series of arguments in which the conclusion of one becomes the premise of another has to be made. Always when one person tries to convince another of the truth of a proposition, he must find one or more propositions on which they both agree. Unless this can be done, argument must be useless. Having ascertained such a basis of agreement, the process must often be a long one, and by a series of inferences involving an equal number of syllogisms before the conclusion is reached.

Reasoning not usually so simple as in the examples given.

Men must find some proposition on which they agree, to reason from, or argument is useless.

Sometimes the main syllogism leading to the final conclusion is formally set forth, and its reasoning is seen to be unimpeachable; but the premises are not admitted by the other party to the discussion. One or both of them in that case must be proved. This implies an argument, and probably a number of arguments, in their support. Thus, if it were a question whether a protective tariff were a proper policy for a nation to adopt, the argument might be formally stated somewhat as follows:

The reasoning may be good, but the premises false.

> All measures that tend to promote home production
> are beneficial ;
>
> A protective tariff does this ;
>
> ∴ A protective tariff is beneficial.

The reasoning here is without a flaw. But the difficulty
would be that the two parties to the discussion are not
agreed on the truth of the premises. Possibly both might
agree to the truth of the major premise ; but the truth of
the minor would certainly be denied by some. Hence,
the necessity of proving it — that is, of proving the minor
premise in the foregoing syllogism. Supposing it to be
attempted in the following syllogism :

> Every policy that increases the number of industries
> promotes home production ;
>
> A protective tariff does this ;
>
> ∴ It promotes home production.

Here, again, the reasoning is correct ; but the opponent
may deny one of these premises — more likely the minor
— which, in turn, must be supported by argument ; and
so on till the parties get back to propositions concerning
which they agree. This will be further complicated by
the fact that in most of our reasoning, even that which is
in form demonstrative, we arrive at conclusions that are
only more or less probable. Hence we prove the proposition we wish to establish, usually, not by a single course
of argumentation, but by several lines, each terminating
in a probability of approximating certainty, the aggregate
probabilities making one still more nearly certain.

KINDS OF SYLLOGISMS.

Syllogisms are divided into **Categorical** and **Hypothetical**.
Categorical syllogisms are such as those we have been

hitherto considering. They are syllogisms in which the premises and conclusions are simple unconditional conclusions.

A Hypothetical syllogism is one in which the reasoning turns on a *hypothesis*, or a *supposition*. A syllogism may contain hypothetical judgments, and yet not be a hypothetical syllogism, for the reason that the inference does not turn upon the hypothesis. As, for instance : **Hypothetical syllogisms.**

> A is either B or C;
>
> D is A;
>
> ∴ D is either B or C.

Here the reasoning does not turn on the hypothesis ; hence it is not a hypothetical syllogism.

Hypothetical syllogisms are divided into **Conditional, Disjunctive,** and **Dilemmatic.**

A Conditional syllogism is one which has a conditional judgment for its major premise, and the affirmation or denial of one of its members for the minor premise. The nature of the conditional syllogism is such that: (*a*) If the antecedent of the major be affirmed in the minor, the consequent must be affirmed in the conclusion. (*b*) If the consequent be denied, the antecedent must be also denied. (*c*) If the antecedent be denied or the consequent affirmed, nothing follows. **Conditional syllogisms.** **Rules.**

> If Mr. Jones is a drunkard he is unfit for a clergyman ;
>
> He is a drunkard ;
>
> ∴ He is unfit for a clergyman.

Here the assertion of the truth of the antecedent necessitates the assertion of the truth of the consequent. But if we put it thus:

> If Mr. Jones is a drunkard he is unfit for a clergyman;
> He is not unfit for a clergyman;
> ∴ He is not a drunkard, —

we see at once that the denial of the consequent necessitates the denial of the antecedent. But if we should deny the antecedent and assert:

> He is not a drunkard, —

we cannot then infer that he is not unfit for a clergyman, because there may be other disqualifications. For instance, he may be ignorant, or fraudulent, or profane — either of which characteristics would render him unfit. So, also, if we assert the truth of the consequent, and say:

> He is unfit for a clergyman, —

it does not follow that he is a drunkard, because, as just shown, there may be other causes of unfitness.

A Disjunctive syllogism is founded on the principle that of two contradictions, one must be true, and the other false. It consists of a disjunctive judgment as its major **Principle of** premise, an assertion or denial of one of the **the disjunc-** members as its minor, and the natural inference **tive syllo-** **gism.** as its conclusion. The disjunction of the major must be genuine; that is, the members must be mutually exclusive. If one be true, the other or others must be false. Thus:

> It is either clear or cloudy, or partly both.

If we assert it is either, then it cannot be one or both of the others.

In disjunctive syllogisms we may reason either from the denial of one member to the affirmation of the other member or members; or we may reason from the affirmation of one to the denial of the others. **Process.**

He either crossed the stream, or he is on this side of it;

He did not cross the stream;

∴ He is on this side of it.

This is an instance of the former, and is called **Modus tollen-do ponens.** *modus tollendo ponens* — establishing one by destroying the other.

He either crossed the stream. or he is on this side of it;

He is on this side of it;

∴ He did not cross it.

This is an instance of the latter method — the **Modus ponen-do tollens.** *modus ponendo tollens*, destroying one by establishing the other.

The Dilemmatic syllogism is one which has for its major premise a dilemmatic judgment, and for its minor a proposition so affirming some member or members of the major as to lay the foundation for an inference. There are three principal forms. **Dilemmatic syllogisms.**

1. The major premise may consist of a single antecedent with a disjunctive consequent; as, If A is B, either C is D or E is F. Affirm the antecedent, A is B, and the disjunctive consequent, either **First form.** C is D or E is F, follows. Deny the consequent wholly, and the antecedent must be denied. If neither C is D nor E is F, then A is not B. If, however, only one mem-

ber of the consequent be denied, nothing follows concerning the antecedent.

2. There may be a plurality of antecedents in the major with only one common consequent. If A is B, X is Second form. Y; and if C is D, X is Y. Or it may be stated in one proposition; If A is B or C is D, X is Y. In this, if both members of the disjunctive consequent, or either one of them, be granted, the consequent follows. But if the consequent be denied, all the antecedents must be denied.

3. There may be a plurality of antecedents in the major, each with its own consequent. In this case, if the antecedents be affirmed wholly, the consequents Third form. must be affirmed wholly; if the antecedents be affirmed disjunctively, then the consequents must be affirmed disjunctively. From the denial of the consequents wholly or disjunctively, the antecedents must be denied wholly or disjunctively.

> If A is B, C is D;
> If E is F, G is H.
> Either A is B, or E is F;
> ∴ Either C is D, or G is H.

Famous dilemma of Demosthenes against Æschines. In the famous oration of Demosthenes for the Crown, he makes a strong point against Æschines, his rival, in this way:

> "If Æschines did not join in the public rejoicings, he was unpatriotic;
> If he did join in them, he was inconsistent;
> But he either did or did not join;
> ∴ He was either unpatriotic or inconsistent."

It may be thought by some that syllogisms of this form contain four judgments; but this is only apparent, since the first two judgments are only different members of the major premise, and can without difficulty be combined in one.

CHAPTER V.

INDUCTION.

OUR definition of reasoning implies that we proceed from established facts to others not previously established or

How we are to ascertain facts from which to reason.

known. But how are we to ascertain the facts from which we are to proceed? This is done by observation and investigation. One of the principal methods of investigation by which we come into possession of facts is **Induction**. For this reason Dr. Hopkins and others place it before Deduction in the order of treatment, and there are no doubt good scientific grounds for following this order. I have not done so, for the reason that the doctrine of inference and reasoning seems to me more easily apprehended in the study of deduction first.

Induction *is the mental process by which we conclude that what is true of certain individuals of a class is true of the*

Meaning of induction.

whole class, or that what is true at certain times will be true at all times.[1] Thus I have seen a great many crows during my life, and have heard of many others. All that I have ever seen or heard of have been black, therefore I conclude that all crows are black. It is in this way that we form a large proportion of our opinions. But it will be seen at once that this is by no means an absolutely certain method of inference. At one time in my life I believed that all swans were white, from the fact that all the swans I had ever seen or heard of were white. Later I have heard of black swans, and have even seen

[1] J. Stuart Mill.

them. It is barely possible that I may sometime learn that there are white crows.

It is true that when we find that a certain quality or fact can be predicated of a considerable number of a class, while no individuals of the class are known of which it cannot be predicated, a fair presumption is afforded that it may be predicated of the whole class. Still, such reasoning is far from conclusive, unless there are other determining principles. *A fair presumption furnished.*

There are two such principles in the application of which we may be definitely certain of our conclusion. One is that in which the conclusion rests on the basis of an enumeration of every individual in the class. Thus, for instance, if a military company is under consideration, and I have ascertained by actual measurement of each man that he is six feet tall, I may assert with entire confidence that the company is composed of men six feet in height. This is called **Formal Induction**. But I do not see anything to be gained in calling it induction at all, or any other kind of inference. It is simply an aggregate of observations. *Two definite determining principles.*

The second principle is that when the *cause* of the quality which we have observed in a few individuals is known to exist in all the individuals of the class, we may certainly know that the quality, or effect of that cause, will be common to all. A familiar instance is that of the planets, which are all presumed to revolve about the sun in elliptical orbits. This is true, not only of those already discovered, and whose orbits have been calculated, but it is inferred to be true of such, if such there be, not discovered. We are confident that when any new planets are discovered hereafter, they will be found *Principle of a common cause.*

to move in elliptical orbits. The reason for this is, that when centripetal and centrifugal forces act jointly on a planet, the resultant must be an elliptical orbit. Hence the conclusion that the orbits of all planets discovered heretofore, or to be discovered hereafter, are in the form of an ellipse. So in all other cases where a particular quality is found to be the effect of a cause which is known to be present in all the individuals of a class, then this quality may be legitimately inferred to belong to the whole class.

There has been a difference of opinion concerning the *underlying axiom* of induction. A certain considerable class

The underlying axiom. have assumed it to be that *Nature is always uniform* in its operations. But this is so far from being an axiom, that it is not only denied to be true by many reputable thinkers, but it has not been believed by the majority of men. Certainly to any who believe in an Infinite Personal Ruler of the universe, it is very far from being a necessary principle. Others assert that the

Uniformity of causation. The axiom. underlying axiom is that of the *uniformity of causation ;* namely, that the same cause under the same conditions will always produce the same effect. This is about as self-evident as any proposition that can be laid down ; it compels universal belief. It will be seen that the second principle of induction presented above harmonizes with this self-evident truth ; or, rather, it is the application of this more general principle to induction.

Dr. Hopkins denies that inductive reasoning can be

Can induction be brought under the form of the syllogism? brought under the form of the syllogism. Other authorities take the opposite view. It seems to me that the latter are theoretically right, though induction, when forced into the form of a syllogism, is a very clumsy, and probably needless, method of presentation. Take the following example : —

> X, Y, and Z are black ;
> But X, Y, and Z represent all crows ··
> ∴ All crows are black.

But in order to prove that X, Y, and Z represent all crows in such a way as to render this inference certain, it would be necessary to make another argument, which, reduced to a syllogistic form, would be something after this fashion : —

> The same cause under the same conditions will always produce the same effect ;
> But the same cause which makes X, Y, and Z black exists in all crows ;
> ∴ X, Y, and Z in this respect represent all crows.

It is probable that some such process goes on in the mind in every case of complete and certain induction. Still very few would care to express it in form, or find any use in such expression. For the more exact kind of induction there are rules and criteria for which we have not space, but which may be found in treatises on Logic.

This exact method of induction is not used much in the common affairs of men, nor even exclusively in scientific investigations. The inductive reasoning among uneducated persons, and to a certain extent among those considerably cultivated, is of a looser, freer kind, but from which great practical results are secured. Thus in ordinary life we judge many objects and events, not with perfect accuracy, and yet with entire confidence, and without misgiving. "We judge of the taste and quality of the food or fruits which we eat,

Exact induction not much used in ordinary affairs of men.

Great practical value of even imperfect induction.

not only by eating one part and inferring in respect to the remainder, but before eating, by an induction founded on the qualities which we discern by our other senses — *i. e.*, by peculiarities of form, structure, color, and smell. We accept or reject, we desire or loathe, that which has not been tried, through our confidence in those carefully observed indications. We do the same with articles of medicine. We do not care to try each fresh piece of rhubarb, or take of every new parcel of arsenic or strychnine, to be convinced by actual experience, that the signs by which we have known the substance to be rhubarb or strychnine show that it will act medicinally, or destroy life. We do not caress a ferocious-looking dog, or come near a horse that makes vicious demonstrations, upon the wise suggestion that experience has not taught us that this particular dog will bite, or this horse kick; but we give both of them a wide berth, on the ground of observation or testimony in regard to others like them. We learn by trial, that certain kinds of soil and certain processes of culture are favorable to the vine. the strawberry, the rose, and the tulip. We derive rules which we assume will always apply to these plants. In the department of science we develop oxygen and hydrogen from a quantity of water, and believe that water, whenever treated in a similar way, will give the same gases. By certain broader assumptions we conclude that electricity causes the phenomena of lightning; that gravitation holds the heavenly bodies in their places, and moves them in their orbits. These various kinds of knowledge are examples, as they are the results of the several assumptions referred to." [1]

Analogy and **Experience** are also involved as bases of rea-

_____
[1] Dr. Noah Porter: The Human Intellect.

soning. Some writers separate these entirely from induction; but they seem to be subsidiary processes Analogy and experience.
rather than independent methods. "In analogy
we reason from individual to individual on the ground of
observed similarity in certain points. . . . In induction
we reason from several individuals and form a class, or
infer a law; in analogy we reason from one or more individuals to an individual, and infer a resemblance in unob-
served qualities or particulars."[1] We have known several
men with a peculiar kind of brogue whom we knew to be
Irishmen. We meet a stranger of whom we know nothing, but we notice that he has the same quality of speech;
we infer that he is an Irishman. We have for years
observed that a storm occurs about the time of the au-
tumnal equinox. We confidently anticipate the recurrence of a similar event in the future years. Still there
are a great many cases in which conclusions from analogy
cannot be drawn with any assurance. Some have gone so
far as to say that the principal use of analogy Use of analogy in estab-
lishing a
possibility.
is in establishing a possibility. For instance, if
a man in maintaining the doctrine of the absolute uniformity of Nature should assert that nothing
which man can do can so affect Nature that she will do
anything which she would not have done if man had done
nothing;—it might be replied that in the growing of
corn Nature does all that is done in the production of the
plant, the ear, and the grain, no matter what man may do.
Man cannot create a single kernel of the corn, nor a single leaf of the stalk, or the tiniest particle of pollen. Still
Nature would do nothing of all this if man should not
furnish certain conditions, such as the preparation of the

[1] Dr. Hopkins.

soil, and the planting of the seed. This may not prove the main point of the negative argument; but it quite *disproves* the subsidiary position of the other party by showing that what he had laid down as impossible is not only possible but actual. It will be found that in many cases of induction, analogy comes largely into play.

Experience differs from analogy in this, that, instead of reasoning from observation merely, we reason from phe-

How experience differs from analogy.

nomena of which we are ourselves the subjects, or, at least, which affect ourselves. True, much of what is called reasoning from experience is really something else. We say frequently, for instance, that we know by experience that fire will burn. This is not true; we only know by experience that fire *has burned* in the past, or possibly that it burns now. We infer from this experience that it will burn in the future. It is on this ground alone that " the burnt child dreads the fire." In much of our common induction, experience is an essential element.

We have already seen something of the operations of the principle of induction in ordinary life, and among

Induction among the uneducated.

uneducated people. They furnish a multitude of inferences which are of great practical convenience, but are not always of any scientific value. " Their results are seen in the common sense and common prudence which are essential to the performance of the common acts and duties of common life. By means of them, men interpret the signs of the material universe, the disposition and acts of the brute creation, as well as the thoughts and feelings of their fellows by looks and actions. Uncommon skill and readiness in interpreting such indications is termed acuteness, discernment, sagacity, tact. Less than the usual sagacity to make such inductions quickly and correctly is denominated slowness and stupidity. The average capacity is called *common sense* in one of the senses of this widely-used appellation." [1]

In scientific induction the process is more difficult. Yet most of the scientific discoveries, great and numerous as they have been, of the last few centuries, have been achieved through this process. The instances are abundant, though not all of them easily understood by the unscholarly mind. The discovery of carbonic acid gas by Dr. Black is a comparatively simple one. Dr. Porter gives the following account of it. He had observed " that caustic lime increased in weight when changed into common lime, and he inferred that this weight must be derived from some agent of or in the atmosphere. This suggested the thought that the other alkalies, being like caustic lime in other properties, were like it also in this. The experiment was tried, and the suggestion was found to be correct. This put him upon the inquiry what the agent was that entered into combination with all these substances. The inquiry resulted in the separation of *carbonic acid gas* as a newly discovered agent, and the determination of its properties and laws." Other equally and some more important results obtained through analogous processes will suggest themselves to many minds; such as the remarkable identification of electricity and lightning by Franklin, Lavoisier's discovery of oxygen, Galileo's, Copernicus', and Kepler's astronomical achievements, and the still more familiar one of Newton's determination of universal gravitation.

Achievements of scientific induction.

Discovery of carbonic acid gas.

[1] Dr. Noah Porter.

CHAPTER VI.

DEMONSTRATIVE AND PROBABLE REASONING.

The difference between these two kinds of proof is as follows:

In **Demonstrative Reasoning** we start with necessary truths. These are abstract statements, and refer to conceptions, and not to realities; and to relations of things rather than to the things themselves. Every step in the argument follows inevitably from the preceding; every conclusion is irresistible.

Demonstrative and probable reasoning.

Probable Reasoning starts from facts, and proves facts. We do not, as in demonstrative reasoning, have intuitive evidence at every step; it therefore admits of degrees of many shades of approximation to certainty, from the slightest probability up to assurance as strong as demonstration. For when we speak of *probable* proof we are not to be misled by the phraseology. The term used to characterize this kind of reasoning is undoubtedly unfortunate; however, if we

The term "probable" liable to mislead.

understand that it is not to be taken in its unmodified meaning, it will answer our purpose. Probable reasoning, while not demonstrative in the sense of giving intuitive or mathematical certainty at every step or in the conclusion, nevertheless may give practical certainty as little disputable as the conclusion of a mathematical demonstration. The man who would deny or doubt the past existence of Napoleon Bona-

It may give practical certainty.

parte or of George Washington would be regarded as not less preposterous or idiotic than he who should doubt or deny that the sum of the three angles of a triangle is equivalent to the sum of two right angles, or that the sum of the squares of the other two sides of a right-angled triangle is equivalent to the square of the hypothenuse.

The evidence in this kind of inference is mainly of three kinds; namely, **Analogy,** **Experience,** and **Testimony.** Of the first two we have already spoken. It is desirable to consider the latter to some extent, though a full discussion of this important subject within the limits of our space is not possible. <small>Three kinds of evidence.</small>

THE EVIDENCE OF TESTIMONY.

The statement of a witness concerning a fact of which he has been the observer, is to be regarded as probable in itself, or unless there be positive reason to the contrary. We naturally believe what is told us. The child has no doubts respecting the veracity of a person who professes to give him information. It is only as one learns by painful experience that there are false statements, that one grows cautious and sceptical. Hence one rule laid down for testing testimony is, that if there is no motive for deception, and especially if there be positive motives for speaking the truth, a witness is to be believed. <small>Statement of a witness probable in itself.</small>

Testimony gathers strength from the substantial agreement of different witnesses having different points of view, and with possibly different biasses or prejudices. It has been said that it is possible to conceive of a number of independent witnesses so great, and so widely differing in character and <small>Substantial agreement of witnesses.</small>

relation to the subject of testimony, that the falsity of that in which they agree shall be mathematically more improbable than the truth of any statement they may make, *whatever it may be.*

LIMITATIONS.

Many things are to be taken into account in estimating the value of testimony. Among these are the reputation **Things to be** of the witness for veracity, the soundness of **taken into** his judgment, his ability to discriminate be- **account.** tween points of importance on which the case may turn, his conscious or unconscious prejudices, the lapse of time between the event and the giving of testimony, the strength or weakness of his memory, the consistency or coherency of his statements, the condition of his powers of perception, etc. It is to be observed that **Possible de-** the witness may be of unimpeachable veracity, **fects of an** and yet he may err in his judgment concerning **honest** **witness.** certain appearances, or concerning the relation of facts, or the time of an event, or the distance, color, size, or other general characteristics of certain objects which are in more or less vital connection with the main subject. The value of his testimony may be impaired by any of these defects. But where none of these exist, where the judgment of the testator is good, his memory **Absurdity of** up to the usual standard, and where there is no **rejecting tes-** evident bias or prejudice, and no discernible **timony where** **no defects** motive to deception, where the testimony of the **exist.** witness is consistent throughout, — especially where it substantially agrees with the testimony of other observers of widely different temperaments and under different conditions, — to conjure up possible doubts and reject all evidence short of demonstration, would be to do away with all knowledge of the past, to make history impossible, and to prevent all progress in science, literature, or art.

CIRCUMSTANTIAL EVIDENCE.

This is a kind of evidence which does not come from the direct observation of witnesses, though its data may, and generally must, depend on testimony. It has already been remarked that all reasoning depends upon the fact that in this world certain events and phenomena are so connected with certain other events and phenomena, that if one of these exists, some other one or more must also exist. The connection may be that of cause and effect, or of some other kind; but it is such that the cognition of one part necessitates cognition of some other part of the connected facts or events. If a stone comes through my window, I know that some force must have impelled it. If I have left a book on my table and stepped out of my room, and on my return the book is gone, I am just as certain that some one has taken it away as though I had been present and witnessed the act. As we say familiarly, and yet not unphilosophically: "It did not go of itself."

Nature of circumstantial evidence.

Dr. Wayland gives some very simple rules governing this kind of evidence, which I take the liberty to transcribe.

Dr. Wayland's rules.

1. "When we are not inquiring for a fact, but for the cause of it, the fact itself must first be established. Thus, if it be required to prove that A murdered B, we must first prove that B has been murdered, and prove it by direct evidence.

2. " In the second place, all the facts on which we rely to prove the fact in question must be established by direct evidence. Thus, if we rely on the facts A. B. D, to prove the fact C, — that is, these facts being proved, that the fact C must have existed, — we must prove the facts A, B. and D by the personal knowledge of the witnesses themselves.

3. " We must show that the facts A, B, and D could not have existed unless the fact C had existed. When we have established these facts, and shown that they can be accounted for on no other supposition than the existence of the fact C, — that is, that unless the fact C occurred, a law of nature has been violated, — then we have proved this fact by indirect evidence."

Application of these rules.

Dr. Wayland goes on to apply these rules in a concrete case.

" B is found alone in a room, dead, stabbed in the back, and his skull fractured by the stroke of a bludgeon. The first thing to be established is that the man is dead ; and secondly, that his death was occasioned by the wounds upon his person; and thirdly, that the wounds could not have been inflicted by himself; that is, that he died by the hand of another, and not by his own. These facts must be proved by direct evidence. It is thus shown that the man was murdered. The question next to be answered is, Who was the murderer?

" Here it is shown that A and B unlocked the door and entered the room together. A noise, as of an altercation, was heard. No one entered the room till A left it, and the first person that entered it after his departure found B dead in the manner described. Now, these facts having been described, it is proved that A is the murderer. B died of these wounds. They could have been inflicted by no person except A, or B himself. They are so situated that B himself could not have inflicted them on himself; they must, therefore, have been inflicted by A."

PART IV.

THE REGULATIVE FACULTY.

CHAPTER I.

NATURE OF THE REGULATIVE COGNITIONS.

In our discussions hitherto we have frequently made use of such terms as "being," "substance," "time," "space," "resemblance," and others of somewhat similar Terms pre- import. But we have not at all considered their viously used, but not ex- origin or their nature. Possibly we have not plained. all observed, what is true, that none of these cognitions have been in any way accounted for among the products of the faculties and powers of the mind that have, so far, come under our notice. They evidently arise from some other power, separate and distinct from all of them. They are very important cognitions, and furnish conditions for most of the knowledge which we gain, and are essential to all profitable and efficient intellectual action. For this reason it might seem more scientific to have discussed them first. Dr. Hopkins does this, following out strictly his policy of taking the conditioning and conditioned successively, and in the order which these words imply. The reason why I have not thought this best for my Reason for purpose is, that the operations and products of not consider- ing these the mind here implied are more abstruse and dif- cognitions ficult of apprehension than the others, and it earlier. seemed better to defer the consideration of them till the pupil should become more familiar with psychologic terms and facts.

As has been intimated. these cognitions do not come to

us through any of the faculties which we have, up to this
time, examined. We do not perceive them;
they are not the product of the Inner-Sense,
though this may make us aware of their existence, as it does of other facts and operations of
the soul. They are not given by the representative faculty, as this gives us nothing which had not been
previously in the mind, and therefore does not account for
their origin. Elaboration cannot produce them, since they
are not directly implied in any of the conceptions or judgments with which this faculty deals; and yet, without these
as a condition, probably most of our reasoning would be
futile. Nearly all modern philosophers have referred them
to a separate power, and the few who have not done so
have found it necessary to treat them as a distinct and
peculiar class of mental products.

They do not come to us through any of the powers previously described.

There are three characteristics of these cognitions which
it is well to bear in mind. 1. They arise from the *energy
of the mind itself.* They are not given through
the senses, nor by the testimony of others, nor
through any process of comparison, abstraction,
generalization, or inference. We simply know them at
once and distinctly; we know them because we are so constituted, and because, when the time comes for us to know
them, we cannot help knowing them, — they force themselves into our consciousness. It is from this fact that they
get the name of *necessary* cognitions or ideas.

They have three char- acteristics.

2. As just intimated, *we know them when the time comes
to know them.* They are under regulation, as well as being
regulative. They have their occasions and conditions, and
come only on these occasions and under these conditions.
They do not arise hap-hazard. There is always a reason

for them, though there is no cause of them save the constitutional energies of the mind. The laws which govern them are as well ascertained and defined as any other scientific principles.

3. The third characteristic of these cognitions is their absolute certainty. There is no knowledge which we ever have that is more certain than these, and most of our knowledge depends for its certainty upon an utter assurance of the truth of these cognitions.

We can perhaps get a somewhat clearer idea of what is meant, by taking **Substance** as one of these ideas, which is never revealed to the mind by any outward or inward observation, and is only known intuitively by the energy of the mind itself. An object is presented to me. I see the color ; by touching it I become aware of a yielding mass, yet not fluid, and of a smooth surface ; also, in connection with sight, perhaps, of the size and shape. I also inhale its odor, and become aware what it is. If I taste it, I shall also perceive its flavor. Now these qualities all appeal to the senses, and through them, as we say, we perceive or know the object. But what is it that we know? Not merely color, odor, flavor, size, and form, but something *to which* these belong, and *of which* these are qualities. This something we do not see, nor hear, nor touch, nor smell, nor taste. We do not cognize it through the senses, nor by any of the means by which we know qualities and characteristics. Still we know quite as well as we know any of those, — probably better, for we may mistake about the qualities, but never mistake about the fact of something in which those inhere. We know that which we call *substance* immediately when

Origin of the idea of "substance."

We know substance quite as well as, and probably better than, we know qualities.

the object is presented. There is no intervening process; it is by a peculiar power of the mind. It is not *caused* by the sensation or the presentation, but these furnish the *occasion;* they are a condition *sine qua non.*

It may seem to many that this cognition of substance is an inference; that it is implied in the fact that qualities

Not an inference. exist; that we cannot conceive a quality without a substance. The last two propositions are undoubtedly true, but they beg the question. How do we know that qualities imply a substance? or why is it that we cannot conceive qualities without substance? It is this very knowledge which is the subject of our present investigation. The mind itself furnishes this knowledge *always*

A necessary idea, and essential to all other knowledge. and *instantly* on the presentation of the qualities. Herein is the necessary character of this cognition, and its essential relation to all other knowledge. Perception is not complete till the mind has furnished that cognition to co-operate with that which comes through the senses.

By **Substance** here is not meant merely *material* substance.

"Substance" not confined to matter. Whatever is the basis of phenomena of any sort, — whether qualities or energies, — that of which they are the phenomena is substance, whether material or immaterial.

CHAPTER II.

THE FACULTY WHICH FURNISHES THESE COGNITIONS.

PHILOSOPHERS are not at all agreed as to the name of this faculty. Dr. Hopkins denies that it is a faculty at all ; and according to his definition of faculty it is not. He limits the faculties to those opera- tions of the mind which are at the command of the will. But he uses the word *power* instead of *faculty*, and it would seem that according to Dr. Hopkins's own philosophy will is implied in *power* quite as much as in faculty. But our nomenclature is greatly defective, not only in this respect, but with reference to certain other psychologic terms.

No agreement as to the name.

Hamilton calls it the **Regulative Faculty,** and this name. seems as good as any, if we are to regard it as a faculty. **Intuition** is a term widely used by some of the best authorities. The only objection to this is that intuition has a wider meaning. As used at present it includes all that knowledge of which the immediate object is the individual, whether given by per- ception, by the inner-sense, or by the energy of the mind itself. It is for this reason ambiguous, and possibly misleading when applied to the source of the cognitions under consideration.

Regulative faculty.

Objection to "intuition."

Reason is adopted by many writers as the proper term to

be used. The objection to this is again that of ambiguity.

Objection to "reason." It is very apt to be confounded with **Reasoning**, and it is very natural from the analogies of our language to think that while Reasoning is the process, Reason must be the faculty which reasons. Still it is one of the terms which has great weight of authority in its favor.

The **Common Sense** was the designation adopted by some of the Scotch philosophers. This would be an appropriate title as representing a power universally possessed by men. The difficulty with it is that the term is pre-occupied with another meaning; namely, "that perception, apparently without a process, by which the average man comes to apprehend the common relations, and to conform himself to the common proprieties of life." Other names have been proposed, but none of them are entirely acceptable. The one we have adopted, the **Regulative Faculty**, seems to be about as unobjectionable as any, and yet it is not entirely satisfactory.

"The common sense."

The cognitions themselves have had names, if possible, still more numerous. The following are some of them : First principles, common anticipations, principles of common sense, self-evident truths, intuitions, innate ideas, *a priori* cognitions, etc.

General names of the cognitions.

These ideas or cognitions, while the first in logical order, are the last to be learned. That is, while they are the condition of all our thinking and knowing, they are yet not easily comprehended, and never definitely understood till the mind has had some discipline and training in absolute thought.

CHAPTER III.

PRODUCTS OF THIS FACULTY.

BEING.

IF an object, say a tree, is presented to my mind, I shall cognize it as something other than myself, and I shall thus not only know the object, but know myself as knowing it. In other words, I shall know both the object and myself as *existing*, and this idea of existence will henceforth connect itself with every object of cognition. It is the idea of **Being**. This is not given by the senses. Through them is furnished to the mind an aggregate of qualities and properties, but the notion of Being is furnished by the energies of the mind summoned to action by the presentation of the object. This idea is a universal attribute of all objects, and hence arises with every cognition of every sort.

Cognition of existence.

SPACE.

When we see any object we simply and instantly know that it is in **Space** and **occupies Space**; that is, as being extended. It would be impossible to cognize a material object, and not think of it as having this characteristic. There has been a difference of opinion among philosophers as to the nature of this cognition. Some writers of great repute regard it as a mere subjective notion, and as having no existence except in the mind —

Cognition of space.

a form which the mind impresses upon outward things.

Space sub-
jective or
objective.
Others of equal repute regard it as an actual entity — not matter and not mind — but yet a condition for matter. This latter expression, "a condition for matter," gives a third class of opinions of eminent thinkers. These regard it not as an entity, and yet as a reality. This reality is involved in the reality of matter. All kinds of measurements, quantifications of matter, all comparisons of bodies with one another, imply this. Long, short, tall, high, low, wide, thick, deep, etc., are so many designations of the space occupied by the bodies to which these terms are applied. Still we could not conceive of space had we not first conceived of occupants of space. It is true, I think, that we do think in a way of space perfectly void, yet in this case we probably use the fiction of impalpable infinitely extended substance, still utterly unlike any other substance.

TIME.

When I see an object as, say, a horse, and my attention is diverted, or the object passes out of my sight, and I either return to it or it comes again within the
Origin of
the notion of
time.
range of my vision; or when I observe some operation of my mind, and note subsequently that this operation recurs, and perhaps repeatedly; or when I see a bird, and then another bird, and still another; there comes into my mind in all these cases the idea of repetition, of succession, and so of duration of **time**. As space is the condition of being regarded as material and extended, so time is the condition of being regarded as in movement or change.

Dr. Brown defines it as the relation of one event to

another, as prior and subsequent. Professor Haven thinks this would imply that it is a mere law of thought, and that it would have no existence independent of the series of events that take place in it. This he disputes, and says: " It is not a mere law of thought, not a mere conception of the mind, not altogether subjective, nor is it a mere relation of one event to another in succession. It is, on the contrary, *necessary* to, and prior to, all successions and all events. It does not depend on the recurrence of events, but the occurrence of events depends on *it*. As space would still exist were matter annihilated, so time would continue were events to cease. But were time blotted out there were no succession, no recurrence, no event. Time is essential not to the mere thought or *conception* of events, but to the possibility of the thing itself." *{Brown's definition. Haven's objection.}*

PERSONAL IDENTITY.

As our cognitions come in succession, and there is an actual lapse of time, memory must be called into exercise. I am certain of events occurring in the past, and I know that I knew them then. But I cannot be certain of past cognitions without *{How this idea originates.}* being certain that the I that recalls the past cognitions, is the same I that was then knowing them. I do not know this by consciousness, for this gives me no knowledge of the past — it cognizes only the present operations of the mind, as perceiving, remembering, etc. We can no more explain it than we explain the cognizance of space and time, but we are as absolutely certain *{Its nature.}* of the fact as it is possible for us to be of anything. This, it must be remembered, is not resemblance or similarity.

These terms always imply two things. But it is of the essence of this cognition, that there is only one and the same thing.

NUMBER.

If we go back to the remarks concerning **Time** we shall see that in the idea of succession and repetition, there is another idea besides that to which attention was particu-

Nature of number.

larly directed. The very fact that we have observed it again, would involve a discrimination between the observations and the times of them as one or two, whether we applied these terms or not. It is the same if we observe different objects of the same general character, as one house and another house, and still others. The idea of **Number** arises necessarily on such an occasion, and it arises from the very constitution of the

Mathematical quantity.

mind, and out of its own energies. Hence all measurements of quantity, all equality, difference, and proportion. Hence, too, the foundation, occasion, and matter of mathematics.

RESEMBLANCE.

When we notice many objects, it is impossible not to observe that some of them are in some respects alike, while others are not. Here arises, by necessity,

The notion of resemblance.

the idea of resemblance and difference. Our first knowledge is of individual objects or energies. We may not, and probably do not, at first, know them to be individual, as the distinction is first made after the process of generalization and classification has gone on for a time, and we have become familiar with general notions. Here, as elsewhere, we know very many things that we do not realize or comprehend. The child does not begin with a section of man or woman or humanity, but with a particular man and a particular woman, calling them father and mother, though not knowing the general term. He sees some other person, and is told that that is a man, and when thereafter he sees another similar object, he calls it a man, but without in the least realizing that he has generalized a class, or formed a conception. Still it is this idea of resemblance as a natural and necessary idea asserting itself in his mind, that is the basis of much thinking and much classification, long before he understands the process or is even aware of its existence. Out of this necessary idea arise all elaborative processes and general scientific methods.

The basis of all classification and all science.

THE INFINITE.

This is not set down here as one of the necessary ideas with which we are now concerned. Some writers have claimed that it belongs here, and I mention it partly on that account, and partly to give the views of those who regard it differently. In the estimation of some of these, this idea arises originally when we think about space, and try to conceive of it as bounded or limited. This we are unable to do. For, whenever we set the limits, no matter how far outside of the material universe — if it have any outside — we draw our enclosing line, we shall inevitably ask ourselves what is beyond this line ; and the answer must as inevitably be, *more space*. Thus we cannot think of space as limited, therefore we are compelled to think of it as not limited or unlimited — that is, **infinite**. This, as we see at once, is a

Not a necessary idea.

negative term in its natural and simple meaning, though we often give it something of a positive signification in our common use of it. It is the not-finite. By the very term we have used, it will be seen that this idea is a product of thought, and not of mere intuition.

By a very easy method we transfer this process and its product to duration or time. We are compelled to think **Transferred** of this as unlimited, as we can conceive of no **to time, etc.** period in the past which was not preceded by duration, nor can we anticipate any future when duration will cease. From these the transference is easy to power, wisdom, knowledge, etc. Says Dr. Hopkins: "The term infinite cannot be applied to either the intellectual or moral attributes of God in the same sense as to space and time. In strictness it can be applied to nothing that admits of degrees or limitation, in any respect. But 'the Infinite' must cover all cases in which the term infinite can be applied. Hence it must be found by comparison, and we shall always be entitled to ask, the Infinite what? This form of expression has its place and use, but, like 'the Unconditioned' and 'the Absolute,' it is so remote from the ordinary lines of thought, and so vague and hazy, that it has special fitness for use when men would 'darken counsel by words without knowledge.'" [1]

SUBSTANCE AND MOTION.

These two ideas are spoken of by some writers as belonging in this category, but by others as not. Of **Substance** I have already spoken, and it seems to me to be cognized directly by the mind as a necessary idea; but it

[1] Outline Study of Man. p. 67.

is so involved in the idea of being, as not to need a sepa-
rate treatment.　Of **Motion** it appears to be Motion as a matter of perception.
enough to say that it is a matter of perception.
It is simply a change of place, or of the relation
of one body to other bodies in space.　Force and power
are implied in it, but they are not it.　Space, of course,
is implied; but motion is not space, nor any modification
of it.　It is not, it is true, a quality of matter in the
proper sense, yet the liability to be moved is undoubtedly
what is sometimes spoken of as a property of matter, and
in this sense, as it seems to me, is perceptible.　Still it is
an open question whether it should come in the list of
original ideas or of those coming through sense-perception.

Besides the ideas which originate from the energy of
the Intellect alone (and I have not undertaken to give an
exhaustive account of them), there are some Other neces-sary ideas.
which are the product of the Intellect and Sensibilities combined, and others, still, which are produced
by the joint operation of Intellect, Sensibilities, and Will.
Of the former are the ideas of *good* (or *happiness*), *beauty*,
the *ludicrous*, etc.; of the latter are *personality*, *freedom*,
causation, *right and obligation*, *merit and demerit*, etc.
Of all these, some discussion will be had in the proper
place in their respective departments.

So far we have been considering original ideas.　There are
also **Original Truths**, or **First Principles**, which are so closely
related to these that many writers fail to dis- First truths.
criminate between them, and thus occasion much
confusion.　These first truths are in the form of judgments
or propositions, and are necessarily true.　"I exist;" "I am
the same man to-day that I was yesterday;" or "I remember that I was in New York last month, and I that remem-

ber am the same person who was in that city;" "The trees that I see are more than one;" "The beating of my pulse repeats itself, and it beats in time;" "Things equal to the same thing are equal to each other;" "A part of a thing is less than the whole;" "The sum of all the parts is equal to the whole;" "Every event has a cause," — these are *truths which cannot be denied.* That is, to deny them would be absurd. An absurdity is a statement To deny these which it is impossible for the human mind to an absurdity. believe, if it apprehends the meaning of the terms in which the proposition is stated. To deny any of these and similar truths, is to violate the principles on which the mind is constituted, and to deny the very conditions of all knowledge.

These ideas and truths must have some marks that distinguish them from others. They are generally given as Distinguish- follows: 1. They are *necessary.* The mind is ing marks of these ideas compelled to know the ideas; it cannot help and truths. believing the truths. 2. They are *universal.* This would follow from their being necessary. But in addition to this, it is a matter of observation. No man has been found who did not assume the truth of these propositions in some way, and who did not show that he apprehended these ideas. 3. They *cannot be proved by reasoning,* for the simple reason that no truths plainer or more evident can be found; and unless this is so, no reasoning can proceed. 4. If a man denies the truth of one of these propositions, or the existence of one of these ideas, he must still act as though he believed it.

DIVISION SECOND.

THE SENSIBILITIES.

CHAPTER I.

GENERAL CHARACTER OF THE SENSIBILITIES, AND THEIR RELATION TO THE INTELLECT.

IT has already been shown that the phenomena of the mind or soul are embraced in three divisions: those of the **Intellect,** of the **Sensibilities,** and of the **Will.** We have just concluded the investigation of the first of these divisions. We now come to the second. *(Tri-partite division of psychical phenomena.)*

The business of the Intellect, as we have seen, is to perceive, to compare, to reason, or, in general, to *know*. It is the function of the Sensibilities to *feel*. The Sensibilities *comprise those powers and susceptibilities of the soul through which all our enjoyment and all our suffering come.* *(Function of the sensibilities to feel.)*

By some writers, the Sensations are reckoned among the Sensibilities. In strict propriety they belong here; but as they are so intimately related to our perceptions, which are purely intellectual phenomena, they have already been fully considered in that connection. It should be remarked, however, that there is a marked difference between Sensations and other phenomena of the Sensibilities. The latter are a consequence of certain phenomena of the Intellect which are an indispensable condition for them. The former, on the other hand, precede the action of the Intellect, and are a condition for *(Difference between sensation and sensibility.)*

its most important, if not its entire, phenomena. They are signs of external things which the Intellect interprets, and this interpretation comprises the main function of perception. Still they are not knowledge, but simply states of the mind, and therefore to be reckoned among the Sensibilities.

The **Sensibilities**, of which we now treat, — leaving out the Sensations, — though entirely distinct from the Intel-

Relation of sensibilities to the intellect. lect in character and functions, are still intimately associated with it. We cannot conceive of any phenomenon of the former which is not preceded by some operation of the latter, and of which the latter is not a condition. It is also probable that there is no action of the Intellect which is not followed by some movement of the Sensibilities. It may not be very marked, nor, perhaps, one of which the subject is clearly conscious; still it is scarcely doubtful that such an effect follows every intellectual process.

The radical element in every production of the combined Intellect and Sensibility is some form of happiness, or of

Some form of good, radical in every product of intellect and sensibilities. something inseparably related to happiness — as Dr. Hopkins would say, some form of *good*. It is true that when the Sensibilities are affected in a certain way, there is suffering; and this would seem to be *an evil* and not *a good*. Still the feeling has reference always to some good, either positive

Evil and good. or privative, as present or absent. Says Dr. Hopkins: " A sensibility is capable of working both ways, perhaps necessarily. As a fact, I think that beings with a sensibility are capable of suffering just in proportion as they are capable of enjoyment. But their suffering is not necessary; it is not that which a sensibility was constituted to give, and therefore we say that the product of a sensibility is a good." [1]

Dr. Hopkins further calls attention to the different meanings attached to the word "good." All enjoyment is good, and that enjoyment always comes from the Sensibility. In this sense everything that can properly be called *a good*, is a product of the Sensibility. Again, there are objects which minister to our happiness and afford us pleasure. We call these *good*, using the word as an adjective. We have also the word *goodness*, which always, I think, when properly used, refers to moral character. This distinction is made between a *good*, and *goodness*, and should always be kept in mind. The former is a normal state of the Sensibilities; the latter, a normal state of the Will.

Different significations of good.

Good and goodness.

The Sensibilities, then, of which the product is some form of good, may be divided as follows: 1. *The Emotions;* 2. *The Appetites;* 3. *The Desires;* 4. *The Affections.*

Division of the sensibilities.

---

[1] Outline Study of Man, p. 196.

CHAPTER II.

THE EMOTIONS.

THE term **Emotion** is used by some writers to cover the whole range of the Sensibilities: the Appetites, the Desires,

Emotion in the broader sense.

and the Affections. It is to be acknowledged that all these are accompanied by emotion, — possibly that emotion is a radical element in them all.

But it is held, at least by many writers, that there is some-

In the narrower.

thing in simple Emotion which distinguishes it from all the others, and certainly something in the others which does not belong to this. Emotion, in its proper sense, is a mere feeling, and, as such, is distinguished from the other products of the Sensibilities by the absence of any craving for any object or any condition. The Appetites are clearly characterized by such a craving. So are the Desires. The Affections, if not so obviously possessing this quality, will, nevertheless, be found on examination to be accompanied by it, if, indeed, it be not a necessary element.

Emotions, then, are *simple feelings arising in the mind*

Definition.

in consequence of some knowledge of certain facts, or some general consciousness of condition.

Such is the emotion of **Beauty**. There has been, in time past, much discussion concerning the meaning of beauty,

Difference as to the meaning of beauty.

and as to that in which it consists. As a simple idea or product it cannot be defined; but we can give such an account of the conditions under which it arises, its causes and concomitants, as to leave no doubt concerning it.

It is used in a *double sense,* and we need discrimination on this account. When we see certain objects, a feeling of pleasure is produced in our minds. There Its double is no accounting for it, except by saying that sense. we are so constituted. This is the emotion of the Beautiful, and I know of no power of language that will more clearly indicate what is meant by it.

But we also look on the objects the cognition of which has occasioned this feeling, and we say they are beautiful. Here there seems to be some external quality instead of a simple feeling, as in the former statement. The real truth is, the one is beauty *subjective,* and the other beauty *objective.* In the one case it is the feeling of pleasure produced by some quality in the object, upon which the attention is fixed. In the other it is the quality in the object, which produces the pleasurable feeling in the mind. This is the difference between subjective beauty and objective beauty.

Beauty is to a great extent ascribed to physical objects, and those mainly apprehended by sight. But it is by no means confined to these. The effect of certain Not confined sounds, and especially of melodies and harmo- to material nies, is precisely the same as that of certain objects. objects appealing to the eye. It is the same also with certain figures of speech, with poetical conceptions, with eloquent utterances, with mathematical demonstrations, and illustrative scientific experiments. So, too, of certain phases of moral conduct, or of dispositions manifested by one individual towards others. We are not to con- Not to be con- found this feeling with that excited by the mere founded with utility of an object or set of objects, or series of utility.

actions, as it is very easy to do. The latter are essentially
different from the former.

The reverse of Beauty is **Deformity**. There are certain
phenomena which produce unpleasant and sometimes painful emotions, and the philosophy of these corresponds to that of the Beautiful, only that the
effects of the former are directly opposite to those of
the latter, and therefore give an opposite name both to the
emotion and to that which is the cause of it.

Deformity.

There has been much dispute concerning *a standard of
beauty*, the question being whether there is any such thing.
It is doubtless true that objects which appear
beautiful to some persons do not appear so to
others. Hence it has come to be supposed by
some that beauty depends entirely upon education, custom,
individual constitution, and association. Unquestionably
these all have much to do in determining the effect of certain phenomena on certain persons. But it does not prove
that there is no such thing as beauty, or any emotion of
the beautiful. Differently constructed musical instruments
may give forth the same harmonies. The same instrument
may also respond very differently as played by different
persons. So the same effect may be produced in the mind
of one person, that is produced in another by a totally different and quite incongruous phenomenon. There is no
doubt that the greatest differences in this respect
result from differences of culture. We know
how the child is delighted with what is not at all
attractive to an older person, and how savages
and persons of little education enjoy pictures and representations which are beheld with indifference, or even positive
aversion, by more civilized and enlightened and better edu-

Is there a
standard of
beauty?

Differences
resulting
from differ-
ences of
culture.

cated people. The former usually are fond of gaudy colors and very pronounced expression and broad presentations, while the latter prefer that which is more subdued, which suggests more than it expresses, and which, by its delicacy, becomes a source of pleasure, though the appeal is always to one and the same susceptibility in each.

GRANDEUR AND SUBLIMITY.

These emotions are very closely akin to that of Beauty. As to the exact distinction between the first two, it has never been satisfactorily given. They are used *Akin to* interchangeably to such an extent by a large *beauty.* number of writers, that it is doubtful if there is any thorough discrimination. It seems to me that almost universally Sublimity is regarded as a loftier emotion than Grandeur. Is it not also true that there is always something of beauty involved in Sublimity, but not necessarily in Grandeur? Further than this the difference is not well defined.

In either case, the feeling is more powerful than that involved in beauty. There is also in it, as is sometimes claimed, a tincture of pain, though, of course, *A more pow-* the pleasure of the effect is greatly predomi- *erful emotion* *than that of* nant. In the case of Sublimity, something like *beauty.* awe affects the mind, and this is akin to fear, — a sort of repression, and, perhaps, slight repulsion. Hamilton gives three forms of Sublimity as affecting the mind: *Three forms* 1. That which is the effect of unusual extension *of sublimity.* in space, — vastness. 2. That which comes from long duration, — eternity. 3. That which is implied in evidences of power.

But the sublime, like the beautiful, is not confined to

material objects. There are instances of moral conduct,
**Moral sub-
limity.** of fortitude, of self-sacrifice and heroism, which
produce the same effect on us as the vastness,
duration, and power evinced in physical scenes. There
have been instances of lofty courage, of voluntary endur-
ance, of patriotic and of moral and religious devotion, in
all the ages, that inspire and elevate the soul which
knows of them, as no vision or sound in the natural world
can possibly do.

THE LUDICROUS.

This is an emotion which it is not only impossible to
define, but difficult to describe. It is readily understood
**Hard to de-
fine, but easy
to appre-
hend.** by every person who has been affected by it. It
is a peculiar kind of pleasure which arises on its
proper occasions. As to what these occasions
are, those who have written on the subject, though agree-
ing in some general features, differ in particular
Its occasions. details. It is generally admitted that there
must be some perception of *incongruity* or inconsistency,
in order to cause this feeling. It must also be unexpected
and uncommon, — there must be the discovery of some
new possible relations. This latter, evidently, would not
of itself be sufficient, as there are sudden revelations and
unlooked-for occurrences that excite far other feelings
than those under consideration. Sometimes indignation
is aroused, and sometimes grief. Frequently in scientific
investigations novel combinations and startling discoveries are made, but they excite no mirth, however intense
the gratification may be. Even the incongruous is not
always ludicrous, especially when the occurrence is of
a nature to endanger life or otherwise harm any one.

Still probably these two elements are nearly always present, and are the main features of what we call a ludicrous scene or event.

This incongruity presents itself in many diverse forms. It may be in objects or in ideas, and in either case it may be accidental or intentional. A little boy dressed in man's clothes, especially if they be of an antique fashion, is usually very ludicrous. A person who has been putting on grand airs and assuming great importance and a rather superfluous dignity, and who, in the very act of displaying these qualities, becomes the victim of some trick or accident in which his dignity suddenly collapses and his importance vanishes, is likely to occasion much merriment. Sometimes this is found in natural objects, as in grotesque formations; or may be represented in art, as in the case of the little marble cherubs trying to drink at a fountain, where one gets behind another and mischievously pitches him into the water. *[Incongruity in diverse forms.]*

The grouping of ideas in such forms as to excite mirth is usually called **Wit**. The definition of this term by the older of our modern philosophers covered a much wider field than that implied in the word at present. The reason of this is that the word itself was formerly nearly synonymous with knowledge or wisdom, as its etymology implies. We have it still retained in some technical forms, as "to wit" in legal documents, where it is equivalent to "know" or to "make known." It may be also said that when the ludicrous utterances of a person are below a certain grade, the title of wit is seldom conceded to them. They may be laughable or comical, or they may degenerate so much as to be called silly, but they are not witty. *[Wit.]* *[A higher form of the ludicrous.]*

Wit has nowhere been so well described as in the following passage from a sermon by Dr. Barrow, which I quote not less for its wonderful aptness of language and marvellous descriptive power, than as a remarkably accurate representation of the subject :

" It is indeed a thing so versatile and multiform, appearing in so many shapes, so many postures, so many garbs, Dr. Barrow's so variously apprehended by several eyes and description. judgments, that it seemeth no less hard to settle a clear and certain notion thereof, than to make a portrait of Proteus, or to define the figure of the fleeting air. Sometimes it lieth in a pat allusion to a known story, or in seasonable application of a trivial saying, or in forging an apposite tale ; sometimes it playeth in words and phrases, taking advantage from the antiquity of their source or the affinity of their sound; sometimes it is wrapped in a dress of humorous expression ; sometimes it lurketh under an odd similitude ; sometimes it is lodged in a sly question, in a smart answer, in a quirkish reason, in a shrewd intimation, in cunningly diverting or cleverly retorting an objection ; sometimes it is couched in a bold scheme of speech, in a tart irony, in a startling metaphor, in a plausible reconciling of contradictions, or in acute nonsense ; sometimes a scenical representation of persons or things, a counterfeit speech, a mimical look or gesture, passeth for it ; sometimes an affected simplicity, sometimes a presumptuous bluntness, giveth it being ; sometimes it riseth from a lucky hitting upon what is strange ; sometimes from a crafty wresting of obvious matter to the purpose ; often it consisteth in one knows not what, and springeth up one can hardly tell how. Its ways are unaccountable and inexplicable, being answerable to the num-

berless rovings of fancy and windings of language. . . .
It raiseth admiration, as signifying a nimble sagacity of
apprehension, a special felicity of invention, a vivacity
of spirit and reach of wit more than vulgar; it seemeth
to argue a rare quickness of parts, that one can fetch in
remote conceits applicable; a notable skill, that he can
dexterously accommodate them to the purpose before him;
together with a likely briskness of humor, not apt to
damp those sportful flashes of imagination. . . . It also
procureth delight, by gratifying curiosity with its rareness
or semblance of difficulty (as monsters, not for their
beauty, but their rarity; as juggling tricks, not for their
use, but their abstruseness, are beheld with pleasure;) by
diverting the mind from its road of serious thoughts;
by instilling gayety and airiness of spirit; by provoking
to such dispositions of spirit in way of emulation or com-
plaisance; and by seasoning matters otherwise distasteful
or insipid, with an unusual and thence grateful tang." [1]

Burnett says, "Wit in writing consists in an assimilation
of remote ideas oddly or humorously connected." Dr. Upham defines it as follows: "Wit consists in sud- Burnett's
denly presenting to the mind an assemblage of statement.
related ideas of such a kind as to occasion feelings of the
ludicrous." Probably the essential thing is in
bringing ideas together in such a way as to sug- Upham.
gest, in a more or less vivid manner, the appearance of
similarities which are *known not to exist*. Sometimes this
is in the form of burlesque, as when objects of great dignity
and importance are described in language usually applied
to minor and insignificant phenomena, as when Hudibras
describes the sun-rising in the following terms: —

[1] Barrow's Complete Works, vol. i. pp. 150, 151.

> ". . . Like a lobster boiled, the morn
> From black to red began to turn."

Sometimes it is in taking insignificant objects or events, and describing them in grandiloquent language, as though possessing surpassing importance. No better instance of this exists, so far as I know, than Irving in "Diedrich Knickerbocker's History of New York," where he portrays the battle between the Dutch factions with all the pomp and circumstance of Homer's description of military operations before Troy.

Irving.

THE DIFFERENCE BETWEEN WIT AND HUMOR.

Wit consists more in the thought and in the language. *Humor* is rather in the manner and form of expression. Sometimes these go together, at other times they exist widely apart. Occasionally humor enhances the wit, or possibly reveals it; for it is possible that a really witty thought may be so expressed that no one, or very few, will perceive it. Also a thought that has no wit may, by the very quaintness of its expression, become very ludicrous. This is done often by the tones of the voice, by particular emphasis, by facial expression, or by some gesture, or a glance of the eye. For the most part humor is found in spoken thought, though it is by no means wanting in written discourse. In the latter it consists wholly, as has been intimated, in peculiarity of expression.

A thought without wit may be made ludicrous by expression.

Humor found more in spoken thought.

It has been asserted by some writers that the ludicrous always implies, in a greater or less degree, in the subjects of the emotion, something akin to contempt for the objects exciting it. It is claimed that, at least, there is in the mind of the former a sense

The ludicrous does not necessarily imply contempt.

of superiority, a looking down upon the object of it. I think this is an error, as almost any intelligent person would perceive who scans carefully his own state of mind on such occasions. It is pure mirth and jollity, and is consistent with the most radical good-will and kindliness. There are, no doubt, instances of the ludicrous where the object becomes contemptible at the same time that he becomes ludicrous, but there is no necessary connection between either the two emotions or the causes of them.

UTILITY OF THE LUDICROUS.

Many persons have the impression that this feeling of the ludicrous is either harmful, or, at least, altogether useless. But we cannot reasonably presume that a characteristic so positive and so universally bestowed is either necessarily harmful or utterly objectless. Like all our other characteristics, it is liable to be abused, and thus become of no good, but a positive evil. There are many reasons for thinking it has to do with the economics of life, and, when kept within its designed limits, it has actual value. *Neither baneful nor useless. Liable to abuse.*

It certainly furnishes relief and refreshment to many minds which otherwise might be hopelessly depressed. It gives buoyancy and cheerfulness, of which there is none too much in the majority of our fellow-mortals. It enlivens and invigorates the spirit often when nothing else will do so. "A merry heart doeth good like a medicine." "He that is of a merry heart hath a continual feast." Genuine wit and humor, acting within their appropriate spheres, are not only ornaments of character, but positive excellences. Even in their painful aspects — for they have these — they have their uses. No one de- *Benefits.*

sires to be the object of ridicule, and this aversion to being laughed at is a powerful motive, where perhaps no other would be effectual in keeping a person from doing foolish and ridiculous things.

On the other hand, a sense of the ludicrous may be strong enough, in minds not balanced by suitable moral restraints and a charitable disposition, to be very mischiev-
Sarcasm a dangerous gift. ous. Sarcasm may be sometimes useful. Occasionally, when a person insists on making himself ridiculous, it is highly important that he should be made to realize his situation. But there is perhaps no power that a man has, which needs to be used with more scrupulous care and greater moderation. Again, there is in some persons a disposition to see all things, even the most serious, in a ludicrous light. Even sacred things are not spared, and sometimes, beyond the intention and consciousness of the subject, it leads to something like sacrilege, if not blasphemy. When carried to this extreme it is not only harmful to society, but the possessor of it suffers serious detriment in the higher and nobler elements of his character.

CHAPTER III.

THE EMOTIONS—*Continued.*

It will have been observed that in all the emotions so far considered, the idea of *good* or happiness has been a constant element. It will be so in not only the emotions yet to be considered, but in all the other divisions of the sensibilities. In so far as this is an idea, and not a mere feeling, Dr. Hopkins places it among the original and necessary ideas which arise from the very constitution of the mind itself. He also places the ideas of beauty and the ludicrous in the same category. He reckons them all as " regulative ideas," differing only from those of the reason, or regulative faculty, in that the latter are products of the Intellect, while these are the products of the Intellect combined with the Sensibility. For this power there is no name in which philosophers agree, and Dr. Hopkins only suggests that of the **Affective Reason,** " meaning by that a reason whose product has the power of affecting us as a motive, which the ideas of the pure reason have not."

Good to be reckoned among necessary ideas.

Also ideas of beauty and the ludicrous.

The affective reason.

This and some other characteristics separate these emotions from those hereafter to be considered. Of the latter we may first proceed to discuss what may be called :

Other emotions differing from the preceding.

THE SELF-REGARDING EMOTIONS.

Cheerfulness is one of these of which no one is ignorant. It is a pleasure not only to the subject of it, but to all *Cheerfulness partly a matter of temperament.* with whom he associates. It is partly a matter of temperament or of constitution. The health and general fortunes of life have sometimes much to do with it. *Joy, delight,* and *gladness* are expressions of this feeling, though they usually refer to the higher and more pronounced forms of it.

The antithesis of this is **Dejection**. Most of us know persons who are chronically unhappy. They carry about *Dejection.* with them a sad countenance, and are habitually melancholy. They see nothing promising in any event or experience of life. If there is nothing of possible evil in the occurrences of the passing day or hour, they insist on interpreting something sinister into them. If the day is cloudy and dismal, they get almost the only gratification of their lives by reflecting that it is just what you might expect. If the day is fair and bright, they are sure it is a " weather-breeder." Their condition comes from a variety of causes — long-continued ill-health, misfortunes, constitutional proclivities, and hereditary tendencies.

Sorrow is a common emotion. This is not to be confounded with habitual dejection and depression. The most *Sorrow not the same as dejection.* cheerful and light-hearted must experience the sorrows of life, and to these the emotion is often deeper than to others. Its occasions are the loss of friends, the evil conduct of those we love, possibly our own wrong-doing, and various others.

There is a group of emotions which we are next to consider, which are closely affiliated, and of which **Self-respect** is the central element. Genuine Self-respect is Self-respect a normal and legitimate feeling. It is the regard described. one has for one's own personality as having in it something of value and importance. It differs from self-love in that the latter is a desire for one's own happiness. Differs from Self-respect in its legitimate action guards one's self-love. own character from degradation, and defends it against all imputations of meanness and baseness of every sort. A man who really respects himself, will not allow himself to do or be what he condemns and despises in others. It gives a dignity and force of character to a man, and few men will respect a person who does not respect himself.

Self-esteem is closely allied to this, and differs from it only in that it is the value and importance at which a man reckons his own personality. It may be reason- Self-esteem. able, sensible, and just, and then forms a basis for the respect which he may properly have for himself. It may also be unreasonable and extravagant, thinking of one's self " more highly than he ought to think." There are instances, though it is to be presumed somewhat rare, in which men under-estimate themselves to their own detriment.

Self-complacency is a feeling that arises when Self-compla- we are pleased with our past conduct, or any cency. particular achievement of our own.

Self-satisfaction is felt when a person contem- Self-satisfac- plates his own excellences, and finds them up tion. to the high standard, or otherwise, which he has set for himself.

Self-sufficiency is the state of mind experi- Self-suffi- enced in view of a person's confidence in his ciency. own abilities.

All these emotions, as intimated, have their normal spheres, within which they are legitimate and healthful. They have also an action which becomes vicious, and hence arise feelings that take on appropriate names.

Pride is one of these. It is an extravagant and abnormal self-respect, accompanied by equally abnormal self-esteem, while the other emotions mentioned are

Pride defined.

likely to be similarly affected and disordered. Pride is thus always to be distinguished from legitimate self-respect. In its strict sense it is a vicious and abnormal emotion arising into a passion. It is also

Distinguished from vanity.

to be distinguished from vanity, with which it is often confounded. Vanity is an inordinate desire for the good opinion of others, as we shall see when we come to it under the head of desires. Pride is an inordinate estimate and regard for ourselves, without respect to what others think of us.

Egotism is pride accompanied by vanity, and manifests itself mainly by obtruding the person of its subject pub-

Egotism as related to pride and vanity.

licly, and rehearsing its own excellences, or fancied excellences and exploits. It thus becomes a very offensive and disagreeable trait to all except its possessor.

Those abnormal developments of the emotions just

Opposite emotions.

mentioned have their opposites, such as humility, self-displacency, self-dissatisfaction, diffidence, etc., all of which imply their character in their names.

Displeasure is a feeling caused by the observance of conduct which we believe to be not only wrong, but injurious to ourselves as well as others. It is not merely the opposite of pleasure, as that would properly be *pain*, but it is a

somewhat positive feeling having reference usually to
conduct. We are not, on the one hand, to con- Character
found it with the malevolent affection of anger ; and causes of
displeasure.
nor on the other to regard it as a moral
sentiment.

Disgust is a still stronger term, denoting the feeling with
which we look upon, perhaps, the same kind of actions
when aggravated by circumstances which make Disgust and
them particularly disagreeable and offensive. indignation.
Indignation is frequently used as synonymous with anger,
but incorrectly, as it regards deeds rather than persons.

SURPRISE, ASTONISHMENT, WONDER.

When anything novel and unanticipated, especially if
it be contrary to our expectations, presents itself to our
minds, a feeling arises, different from any of Difference
those previously mentioned. This is **Surprise.** between surprise and as-
Astonishment indicates a higher degree of the tonishment.
same kind of feeling, with, perhaps, a tendency to repress
the ordinary action of the mind. When the object is
dwelt upon for any considerable length of time, and ex-
cites a certain degree of inquiry, with perhaps some sense
of mystery, the feeling excited is called **Wonder.**
These emotions are of use to us, since they Wonder.
often cause us to pause and consider. We are thus also
led to investigate and ascertain facts and principles before
unknown. We frequently, as a consequence, take meas-
ures for our defence and security, as well as to make
improvement in many ways. Wonder has sometimes been
called " the seed of knowledge."

The feeling of **Reverence** arises when we have knowledge of persons of great dignity and moral worth, or

The kind of persons for whom reverence is felt. authority, or of extraordinary learning or genius, who have used these powers for the advancement of virtue and religion in the world. Every generation and every nation have a few such; and the masses of men, as they contemplate the characters of these persons, are affected by this emotion. No man, unless wanting in certain essentials of desirable character, would fail to be affected in this way, by the mention of such names as those of Abraham, Moses, St. Paul, St. Augustine, Howard, Wilberforce, Washington, and a host of others who have died, as well as of many who are now living. A moderate degree of this feeling is called *respect* and *regard*. A high degree, such as is felt for the very noblest and most godlike of the race, is *veneration;* and that feeling with which we regard the Infinite and All-wise Creator, is denominated *adoration.*

HOPE AND FEAR.

It is some matter of doubt whether this is the precise place in which to consider these two emotions. Indeed, it

Doubt concerning these emotions. is disputed by some that they are, in strictness, simple emotions at all, there being in each an intellectual element. But there is, at least, an emotional element also. They may, perhaps, better be classed here than anywhere else.

Hope comprises both an expectation of a thing, and a desire for it. The resultant is a feeling of pleasure. There

Meaning of hope. are, of course, different degrees of hope; sometimes it is of the feeblest character, and again of the strongest and boldest, approximating perfect confidence. It is one of the most effective motives of action, and a person's character and success in life are determined very largely by the place this occupies. Its utility. It encourages effort and inspires great deeds; it also supports the soul under the severest trials and hardships. It anticipates pleasures and prosperities in the future, when there are none in the present. Its anticipations sometimes take the place of joys that never come.

> "Hope springs eternal in the human breast;
> Man never is, but always to be, blest."

Fear has two significations. One of these makes it the opposite of Hope. It is thus made up of expectation and negative desire, or aversion. We fear that Significa-
tions of fear. which we expect, but desire not to be. This, like hope, has different degrees. It may be a mild disquietude, or it may be utter despair, and thus in peculiar instances exceedingly distressing.

Fear in its other signification is the feeling we have in view of something certain or possible to come into our experience. It is the state of mind which is Being afraid. meant when we speak of being *afraid*. Children are afraid of the dark or of strangers. Older persons are afraid of certain other persons because of their character, or of certain possibilities of conduct in them as affecting those brought in contact with them. In Not the exact
opposite of
hope. this sense it is not the exact opposite of hope, though there is usually something of expectation in it. In its more serious forms it becomes *dread*, and deepens into *alarm* and *terror*. The last term expresses a condition in which one partially or wholly loses self-control by the intensity of the fear. It is distinguished from

despair by the condition of violent agitation and excite-
ment which characterizes it, while the characteristic of the
latter is lifelessness, and resignation to fate. Still we
sometimes speak of one's being "paralyzed by terror."

Horror.
This doubtless indicates the physical rather than
the mental effect. *Horror* represents a cognate
feeling to fear and terror, but perhaps differs mainly in
this, that we may fear and be in terror of that which is not
in itself hideous or repulsive. In horror there is always
a pronounced element of detestation, a shrinking from the
object or act as something unendurable and abominable in
itself.

CHAPTER IV.

THE MORAL EMOTIONS.

THIS is not the place to enter extensively upon the subject of Ethics, but a few words may be necessary in order
to put our immediate topic in its proper light. Relation to
It is to be taken for granted that the words ethics.
right and *wrong* have a definite and well-understood meaning, and that they refer to certain classes of actions. By
the use of our intellectual powers we ascertain whether an
action is right or wrong, just as we determine what actions
are wise and what are unwise, what are healthful or un-
healthful, graceful or awkward. In making this estimate
of moral conduct, there must be taken into account circumstances, conditions, motives, intentions, etc., as there
are comparatively few acts the moral character of which
is the same in all cases. The moral emotions Occasions of
arise on the contemplation of actions thus deter- moral emo-
mined as right or wrong. In observing a right tions.
action there is a distinct feeling of approval; in an opposite
instance there is an equally distinct feeling of disapproval.

There are three cases to be considered: Three cases.
1. When a person determines that a certain
action is right for him to do, and wrong not to do. In this
case there is a feeling of *obligation*, an impulse Obligation.
to do it, inclining him towards the right and
away from the wrong. It will be noticed that this feeling
is consequent upon the determination or judgment concern-

ing the character of the act, and is no part of that judgment. It is a natural and inevitable consequence of that
judgment. This, it seems to me, is the peculiar and essential function of **Conscience**. Indeed, it may be
doubted if there is any other function which
can be shown to be so closely connected with this as to be
properly regarded a modification of it. There is certainly
no need that Conscience do the judging and reasoning
which are here implied, since the same faculties which
usually do the judging and reasoning about other matters
are fully competent for the same office here. In this view
of Conscience as a simple impulsive faculty or
force, we have a power that acts uniformly and
universally, and which is also, in its proper
sphere, infallible. That is, *it always impels us to do what
we judge to be right, and not to do what we judge to be
wrong.* It does this if it does anything. It may be so
misused or abused as to become inactive, or we may so
habitually disregard its monitions that at last we cease to
feel them; but whenever its voice is heard at all, it always
urges to do what one's judgment and reason approve as
right, and it does this in all men.

2. When we have done a wrong act, the consequent
emotion is one of *disapproval*, and when we have acted
rightly, it is one of *approval*. The former consequence is more conspicuous than the latter,
inasmuch as it is more natural to do right than
to do wrong; and therefore we do not notice the effect, it
is so much a matter of course, unless it be in a case where
great temptation to act wrongly has been resisted. The
connection of this phase of moral feeling with the previous
one is obvious. In both the sense of obligation, of ought

Conscience.

*A simple im-
pulsive
faculty.*

*Feeling of
disapproval
of a wrong
act.*

or ought not, is present; in the former, as something to be complied with, an imperative which we are not at liberty to disregard; in the latter, as something which has been violated, and which consequently brings pain and condemnation, — a sense of guilt and ill-desert.

3. There is, in the third place, the feeling we have when we observe the right or wrong actions of others, — of approval if they do right, and disapproval if they do wrong. There is in the latter no sense of self-condemnation, but the feeling probably arises from the reflection that if we were in the place *(Approval or disapproval of acts of others.)* of the persons observed we should have this feeling, and therefore we condemn their conduct as we would have condemned our own. It is, as in the first case, a disapproval or approval, as the case may be, of conduct in others which has been first realized in our own experience.

There are several terms representing the feelings implied in Conscience, or more or less closely affiliated with it. They are Repentance, Penitence, Contrition, Compunction, and Remorse.

Repentance is a general term indicating regret and sorrow for certain actions and courses of conduct, and a disposition or purpose to do the opposite in the future. *(Repentance and penitence.)* **Penitence** is more usually expressive of this feeling in relation to religious conduct. **Contrition** is nearly synonymous with penitence, but has in it more conspicuously the element of humiliation, and *(Contrition, compunction, and remorse.)* also of affection towards the being offended as enhancing the sorrow. **Compunction**, as the name implies, is a pricking and goading of conscience, — the uneasy and painful feeling resulting from the violation of obligation. **Remorse** is the same feeling in a more settled and oppressive form, a positive sense of guilt tending towards hopelessness. It will be noticed that Compunction and Remorse differ from the others in this, that they have no element of purpose of change in them. They are pure emotions consequent upon evil conduct. The others are not pure emotions, but are combined in some measure with the action of the Will.

Faith is also largely emotional, though having in it something of the element of both the intellectual and the voli-
Faith. tional. It is based upon belief, and implies a purpose; but it also is characterized by a feeling of confidence and trust in another, or in something extraneous to self.

CHAPTER V.

THE APPETITES.

PASSING from the consideration of the Emotions, we come upon a new range of sensibilities known as the **Appetites** and **Desires**. I mention them together, as they have something in common which distinguishes them from the simple emotions. The latter are the effects of some intellectual operations, and do not themselves, at least directly, incite to action. But in this new field the feelings that we cognize do impel to action. They are what Sir William Hamilton calls *conative*, inducing effort on the part of their subject. Indeed, he puts them in the department of the Will, and treats them accordingly. But most writers class them in the category of the Sensibilities.

How appetites and desires differ from emotions.

The Appetites and the Desires have this in common, that they are both cravings for something that the subject of them lacks. For this reason some writers have included both under the one head of Desires; while some others, mostly ancient philosophers, have reckoned them all as Appetites. But at present they are divided on what seems to be a clearly intelligible and reasonable principle, namely, that the one class refers to the wants of the body, and the other to those of the soul.

What they have in common.

The *Appetites, then, are those cravings of the mind which*

relate to the well-being of the body. They have been de-

Appetites
defined.
scribed by some writers as *physical* feelings, but, as it seems to me, unreasonably. There are properly *no* physical feelings, since all feeling of any sort is in the mind, not in the body. Cut off all connection of any part of the body with the brain and the mind,

Have their
causes in the
states of the
body.
and there is no feeling at all in that part of the body. Still these feelings have their causes in the conditions of the body, and this is one of their chief characteristics. Another mark of the Appetites

Their perio-
dicity.
is their *periodicity*. They act at intervals, and with a certain degree of regularity. They are also accompanied by an uneasy sensation. They differ from instincts in this, that they are to a certain extent under the Judgment and Will.

The Appetites as usually given are Hunger, Thirst, and the craving for Air and Sleep. To these are added by

Kinds of
appetites.
many authorities, the Sexual appetite, and the desire for Exercise. "If we would know how many appetites there are," says Dr. Hopkins, "we must inquire how many things there are, generically, that are necessary for the well-being of the body, and we may be sure there will be within the body a craving for these things."

The end of the Appetites is not mere sensual gratification. They are designed for the preservation of the body,

Object of the
appetites.
and the perpetuation of the race. There is, of course, a gratification in meeting these demands; were this not so, the design would be frustrated. Except for the pleasure there is in eating and drinking, thousands of persons would so frequently neglect these wants of their nature as to destroy their health and life.

The Appetites are self-limiting. In a man of normal condition, whose Appetites have not been abused, they crave no more than a healthful satisfaction. The great danger is in the gratifying, not the Self-limiting. appetite beyond this point, but another desire closely associated with it. For instance, in eating certain kinds of food, in addition to the gratification of the appetite, there is a pleasure to the palate and other organs of taste. A desire is created for the continuance of this pleasure, and eating is sometimes continued for this purpose after the appetite itself has utterly ceased its demands. This leads to over-eating, and thus to bodily harm, and may grow into a most evil habit.

This is found to be the case especially in *artificial appetites.* There are many articles of food and of drink for which there is no natural craving. An appetite Artificial for them, however, can be cultivated. It is appetites. probable that nothing is ever gained by their cultivation, since, as Dr. Hopkins says, it is pretty nearly certain that in the constitution of man, God gave him as many appetites as would be good for him. These artificial appetites, too, are frequently, if not always, more difficult to govern than those which are natural. Take, for in- Narcotics. stance, the use of tobacco. Probably no person, unless inheriting abnormal conditions, ever liked tobacco in any form. It is, without much doubt, naturally universally offensive. Yet, the taste once acquired and the appetite cultivated, it easily becomes a dominant passion, hard to shake off, even when known to be undermining the health and ruining the constitution of its victim. There are thousands who would gladly give a great sum to free themselves, without the necessary personal sacrifice, from the dominion of this pernicious appetite; but the effort is so great that rather than make it they continue to submit to its thraldom.

What is true of this and other narcotics is true in a still more deplorable degree of the appetite for alcoholic beverages. It begins to be created in the pleasant stimulus of this substance acting on the system, and the reaction from which begets a stronger craving, the gratification of which causes a greater stimulus, and thus, gradually, there is an overmastering power established among the physical elements, which in no long time renders the subject a helpless victim and slave to its imperious demands.

Alcoholic beverages.

It is true that men do become the victims of appetites which were originally normal and healthful. We read, and perhaps know, of gluttons and gormandizers. They have become so, not by the natural use of their appetites, but by an artificial indulgence of them. There are other ways in which appetites are created so as to have all the effect of artificial cravings, by ministering to the palate at unseasonable hours, when the natural appetite itself makes no sort of demand, and that too, for articles not in themselves unwholesome, and for which, in a limited degree, there is a normal appetite; and thus untold harm is done to the health and strength of the individual.

Normal appetites becoming abnormal.

INSTINCTS.

This is perhaps as good a place as any to consider the subject of the *Instincts*, since, though differing radically from the Appetites, they have a certain relation to them, and at one or two points are very similar to them.

Instinct, according to Reid, is "*a natural blind impulse to certain action, without having any end in view, without deliberation, and very often without any concep-* Definition of *tion of what we do.*" "An instinct," says Paley, instinct. "is a propensity prior to experience, and independent of instruction."

When Reid says, as above, that instinct is without any end in view, he doubtless means that the subject of the instinctive action has no end; for unquestion- No end, so far ably the action is always directed to some end, as the sub- and its end is always the well-being of the ject is con- individual or of the race. Instinct is repre- real end sented as unintelligent. This is true so far as nevertheless. the subject is concerned, but that the most far-seeing in- telligence is in some way involved cannot be Intelligence doubted. The Creator of the subject has fore- implied, but seen, and by marvellous wisdom provided for, subject. the operation of instinct. If instinct were like intelligence it would imply far more wisdom in the bee and the spider, and many other animals, than in man. The sitting hen turns over her eggs by ruffling them, in order that the yolk, the specific gravity of which is greater than that of the white, may not rest on the shell, and thus prevent the growth of the chick. Here, evidently, is intelligence, but not the intelligence of the hen. She would not know an egg of her own from a glass egg, and would sit upon a nest full of the latter as contentedly as upon the former. A beaver constructs a dam which can scarcely be beaten by a civil engineer; but if shut up in any place destitute of water, and furnished with materials, he will construct just as good a dam as though putting it across a stream, — a dam, of course, which could have no object. It is

characteristic of instinct, that it is incapable of improvement or development.   There is incalculable
Incapable of
improvement. progress in man's architecture and mechanical
talent, from the cave dwellings and rude huts of the primitive races to the neat edifices and sumptuous houses of
modern times; but the bee builds its cells precisely as it
did five thousand years ago. So of the nests of birds, the
ball of the silkworm, and many other structures.

But we are concerned here with the instincts of **men**,
and not those of the lower animals, except as the latter aid
us in understanding the former. It is to be remarked that
Inverse ratio
of instinct
and intelli-
gence. the relation of instinct to intelligence is that of
an inverse ratio. When the former is at its
maximum the latter is at its minimum, and *vice
versa.* Dr. Hopkins and Dr. Chadbourne have both illustrated this by the accompanying simple diagram; namely,

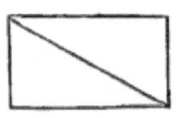 that of a rectangle divided diagonally into
two triangles, one representing instinct and
the other intelligence. At the lower part
of the upper triangle, representing intelligence, the latter becomes virtually nothing, while instinct
occupies the whole space. The same is true of the upper
point of the lower triangle, representing instinct; there
the latter is *nil*, while intelligence occupies the whole
space. So at every intermediate point, the wider the
intelligence the narrower the instinct, and *vice versa.*

It is in accordance with this principle that we find the
instincts more numerous and more active in children than
Instincts of
children. in adults. The newly-born infant sucks and
swallows its food as perfectly as if it knew all
the principles of the operation. Sucking and swallowing
are very complex operations. Anatomists describe about

thirty pairs of muscles that must be employed in every draught. Of these muscles every one must be served by its proper nerve, and can make no exertion but by some influence conveyed through that nerve. The exertion of all these nerves is not simultaneous. They must succeed each other in regular order, and their order is no less necessary than the exertion itself. This regular train of operations is carried on according to the nicest rules of art by the infant who has neither art, nor science, nor experience, nor habit." [1]

The most intelligent men, up to old age, do some things entirely by instinct, and other things occasionally under the same impulse. Certain of our instinctive operations we learn by observation, and sometimes find out how to control and modify them.

Men do certain things entirely by instinct.

[1] Dr. Reid, quoted by Dr. Upham.

CHAPTER VI.

THE DESIRES.

The Desires have the same relation to the well-being of the mind that the Appetites do to that of the body. We
Desires de- have seen that if we could know how many
fined. generically different things were requisite to the well-being of the body, we should know how many appetites there are. So it is with the desires and the well-being of the mind. It will be seen that the Desires are of a higher order of sensibilities than the Appetites. There are several kinds of Desires, each having its distinctive
Self-preser- designation. First among these is the desire
vation. for **Continued Existence**, or **Self-Preservation**. No principle is naturally stronger in man than this. We do not need to prove this. It is obvious in the conduct of all men, whenever they are exposed to danger. Under certain conditions, it may be overcome by other principles temporarily gaining the ascendency, but it can hardly be said, even in these instances, to be extinguished.

The action prompted by this desire is two-fold. It may be either *instinctive* or *voluntary*. The former takes
Two-fold place when life is threatened or imperilled by
action. sudden emergencies. When a person is in danger of falling, he instinctively puts forth his hand to save himself. When a blow is suddenly aimed at him, he instinctively makes an effort to ward it off. Such a provision seems to be made for man, to serve in cases where

calculation and adaptation of means to ends could not be made available in time. When there is opportunity for consideration, the action prompted by **Voluntary.** the desire is said to be voluntary. This action is usual in self-defence.

DESIRE OF PROPERTY.

There is a natural craving of the mind for *possession*. The assurance of continued existence is followed by a desire for means of supporting that existence, and making it comfortable and agreeable. Hence we find in all men the craving for possession of that which would maintain life in greater or less abundance. It is the mainspring of all industry, of all production, of nearly all invention and enterprise. Civilization depends largely upon it. It is one of the most powerful propensities of the human mind. While innocent and most useful within its legitimate limits, it may be easily carried beyond those limits by its own momentum, and become a great power of evil in the world.

DESIRE FOR KNOWLEDGE.

The third of these desires is known as the **Desire for Knowledge**, or **Curiosity**. This is a normal characteristic of our constitution. We are made to crave knowledge, and are furnished with means and instru- **Curiosity.** mentalities by which this may be acquired. We see the principle in operation everywhere. In the most ordinary community, let any new and strange event take place, and everybody is agog to know all about it. It is of the highest utility, and furnishes the spring to the **Its utility.** greatest achievements in science, literature, and art. Under its stimulus have taken place the wonderful explorations, expeditions, and experiments for the purpose of extending the area of human knowledge.

DESIRE OF POWER.

This is also a normal and legitimate feature of our constitution. We see it in its purest and simplest form *In children.* sometimes in children. There is great joy in a boy's mind when he has achieved something which he has found it difficult to compass. The mere knowledge of certain kinds of ability, wholly independent of any ulterior good, is itself a very positive satisfaction. *May be abused.* It is also a proper object of effort. It is one of the great duties of man to acquire as much power as he can justly. Like all other great gifts, power is liable to be abused, and is pretty likely to be, if not kept in subjection to moral principles.

> "Oh, it is excellent to have a giant's strength;
> But it is tyrannous to use it like a giant."

When this desire becomes excessive, and is cultivated for selfish ends, it is called **Ambition**. It is simply an inor- *Ambition.* dinate desire of power, not as a means to noble and worthy ends, but because it will promote one's self-interest.

DESIRE OF ESTEEM.

This is another natural and universal principle of our constitution; that our friends, and people generally, *Its utility.* think well of us, is an occasion of simple and innocent gratification. It begins with us in infancy, and is never wholly wanting in the most advanced age. It is not a mere pleasure; it has also its positive utility. Unless we have the approbation of our fellow-men, we can do them little good; and to be deprived of this is a great deduction from our usefulness. Not necessarily selfish. It is by no means necessarily a selfishly prompted desire. In circumstances where, so far as we can see, this approval will in no way affect our business, or our general reputation, or any of the enterprises of life to A good in itself. which we devote ourselves, we still hunger for it for its own sake. If we happen to be set down for only a brief space among entire strangers whom we shall never see again, and who can do us neither good nor harm, still we should be sorry to know that, without conscious cause on our part, we had incurred their ill-will. To care nothing for the opinion entertained of us by others, or to so pretend, indicates a low and unworthy moral character. It is not merely for the present that we are animated by this desire. We are not improperly solicitous that our memory after we are dead shall be held in respect, or, at least, not in dishonor.

This, like other desires, has its appropriate limits, within which it is innocent and wholesome, but beyond which it is unwholesome and harmful. When Limitations. it becomes thus inordinate and abnormal, it is called **Vanity**. It is always a foolish and undignified senti- Vanity. ment, even in its most common forms; in its excessive action it becomes offensive and repulsive.

DESIRE OF SOCIETY, HAPPINESS, AND LIBERTY.

There are still other forms of the sensibilities which have the general characteristics of desire, and by some eminent

writers are placed in this list. Others, for certain reasons,
do not so reckon them. They are the *Desire*

Doubtful if
they are to be
classed here. *of Society,* the *Desire of Happiness,* and the
Desire of Liberty. The *Desire of Society* appears
to be very much of the same general nature as the other
desires already described. We are constituted so that
society is essential to our individual welfare. No man is

No man suffi-
cient to him-
self. ever made to be sufficient to himself. The full
complement of things needful for his welfare is
never in any one individual. All the members
of a community are interdependent. Each has something
that others, probably many others, lack and need. Hence
this desire is as clearly natural as any other which comes
under our consideration. The only reason I have seen why
it should not be reckoned among the original desires is
that given by Dr. Hopkins, namely, that "it is so far some-

A condition
men are born
into. thing that we are born into, and a condition for
the gratification of other desires, and for the
exercise of the affections and higher faculties,"
that we prefer to place it in a list somewhat separated
from the more general desires. This distinction is doubtless worthy of consideration, if not wholly determinative.

The *Desire of Happiness,* or, as Dr. Hopkins would say,
of *Good,* is what is generally known as *Self-love.* There
is a clearly marked difference between this and the other
desires. That it is a craving for something not in possession, and is consequently a great impelling force, is very
evident. So far it is similar to the other desires. It differs

How it differs
from other
desires. from them in this: that it can get no direct
gratification, and none at all except through the
operations of the other desires. Suppose all
the other desires to cease, and only the desire of happiness

to remain. This cannot be gratified until some one or more of the other desires revive. Some such state as this does occur at certain times to some persons, and it is a most distressing condition. It is the state denominated Hypochondria, a state in which, while there is Hypochondria. a craving for good or happiness, there is no conceivable way in which this good can come. The reason of this is, that there is in this condition an absence of any desire the gratification of which gives pleasure; and a more hopeless and melancholy situation can scarcely be imagined.

"The *good* does not lie proximate to the will. It is the common result of all forms of activity, when the objects directly chosen are attained. Entering thus as Good does not lie proximate to the will. a common element into all desires, it cannot be classed in the same rank with any one of them. It has, indeed, the same relation to all specific forms of desire, that consciousness has to all the other mental operations. It is something different from any one of them, it is common to them all, and is that without which no one of them could be." [1]

There is a clear distinction between self-love and selfishness, to which particular attention is called, as it is not always made by writers and speakers of culture. Self-love and selfishness. Self-love is a simple, natural, and legitimate desire, such as all men properly have. Selfishness is *inordinate* self-love — self-love passing beyond its legitimate limits, and overmastering more important desires and motives.

The *Desire of Liberty* differs from the general desires in much the same way as the desire of happiness, though not,

[1] Hopkins's Outline Study of Man.

perhaps, to the same extent. It has certainly a peculiar re-

Relation to the particular desires. lation to those desires. It may be rudely stated somewhat thus: it is a desire for the gratification of all other desires. We do not like to have our desires restricted in any way, and any repression of them, or prevention of their gratification, we regard as a limitation of our liberty. I suppose a child or an uneducated person

A simple definition. would define liberty as having and doing everything one wishes, and having and doing nothing else; and probably it cannot be much more clearly defined. But it will be seen by this that the desire for liberty can hardly exist independent of other desires. Were these not in existence, probably the craving for liberty would never be felt. Hence, while the element of desire is the prominent feature here, it is evident that, like the desire for good or happiness, it is separated by other characteristics from the desires first spoken of.

CHAPTER VII.

THE BENEVOLENT AFFECTIONS.

THE Affections differ from the Desires in that they are more complex, and also of a higher character. The element of desire is prominent in them, but it is accompanied by another element. When we have an affection for certain persons, there is not only a craving for their society, but we have in addition, a disposition to please them, and to do what they would desire to have done. This feeling becomes so strong where the affection is great, that it subordinates all other considerations. The property, the preferences, and even the life itself of the subject, are readily sacrificed for the benefit of the object of the affection. So, on the other hand, if an aversion is from any cause felt for a person, we do not desire association with this person, and the natural impulse is not to do him any favor, but rather the contrary. Unless overborne by other considerations, as it is in wise and charitably disposed individuals, the spontaneous impulse of the mind towards such a person is to do him some harm.

How affections differ from desires.

Aversion.

The Affections have been classed by a majority of authorities, as **Benevolent** and **Malevolent**, accordingly as we regard individuals favorably or unfavorably — as we *love* or *hate* them. This division has been objected to by Dr. Hopkins, on the ground that these two words imply the action of the Will; whereas these

Classifications.

are natural sensibilities, and exist before the Will is so fully constituted as to control them, and, in fact, before the Will is called into action. He says, in animals there is no malevolence. The beast of prey has none of this feeling towards his victim. "He does not hate him; he simply wishes to eat him." Dr. Hopkins would call these **Beneficent and defensive or punitive.** Affections which lead to the doing of good, *Beneficent;* the opposite feelings and impulses he would call *Defensive* or *Punitive*, inasmuch as in the lower animals this seems to have been the reason why they are constituted with these dispositions.

But as we are dealing with men and not with brutes, and as the manifestations of these feelings are quite different in the latter from what they are in the former, these seem to be awkward and unsatisfactory designations, and not at all clearly antithetic to the name given to the opposite affection. If *Beneficent* is a better term than *Benevolent* **Why not maleficent?** as applied to the one, why would it not be better to call the other by the name of *Maleficent?* This would at once give a natural and easy distinction, and would also adequately describe them. But on the whole, and notwithstanding the reasonableness of the objection to the present nomenclature, I prefer to adhere to it till the higher authorities are agreed on something better.

The further division is made of the Affections as *Natural* and *Moral.* The former are those which spring up spon- **Natural and moral.** taneously, and are not under the control of the Will. They are found in brutes as well as in men. The latter are under control of the Will. This distinction will not call for a separate treatment of the two classes of affections.

The Benevolent Affections assume a variety of forms, according to their respective objects. These may be grouped under the heads of *Love of Kindred,* Different forms. *Love of Country, Friendship, Love of Humanity,* *Gratitude,* and *Sympathy.*

The word *Love* is, in our language, made to cover a large range of conceptions, to many of which it is, in strict propriety, altogether inapplicable. A boy loves Use of the word love. his play and his instruments of amusement; some men love horses and dogs; a girl loves parties, and beautiful dresses and adornments; the scholar loves study;. certain persons love a fight; and others love particular kinds of food and drink, and exciting scenes. Now clearly these uses of the word *love* indicate only a delight and pleasure in the possession or observance of these objects or events, and they are mostly of a physical character. But we do not really *love* these things; we simply *like* them. Love in its proper sense must have a Purely personal. personal object. It is a purely personal feeling, both as to its object and its subject. This is clear from what has already been said of the nature of the Affections, namely, that they imply a desire on the part of the person who loves, to please and benefit the object loved. Let us consider the several forms of the Affections.

THE LOVE OF KINDRED.

This is the earliest and most primitive of the natural affections. **Parental Love** springs up at once, as soon as the fact of parentage is realized. I do not mean Earliest and most primitive. Parental love. that it exists in its full strength, but it is in the soul at first, and grows and deepens, and becomes more and more controlling with the increasing age of the object. How powerful it often is, need not here be illustrated, since every person may find instances in great numbers within the circle of his own observation. The love of a mother for her child has become the simile and standard of all great affection that is found in humanity; and the toil and hardship, and the uncounted and unmeasured sacrifices to which she will subject herself, prompted by this love, have been rehearsed a thousand times, in story and in song, in all the literatures of the world.

This is mainly instinctive, as appears from the fact that it is a natural affection. It is akin to the intense interest

Mainly instinctive. that the lower animals have for their young. It is, nevertheless, capable of taking on a moral character. It may be made the subject of consideration, and be brought under moral rules. There are also exceptional instances in which the affection has been alienated, and indifference has taken its place. In such cases ethical motives and obligations may be presented as a means of reviving and restoring it.

The utility of this affection is seen in the consideration that without some such sensibility parents might not be

Its utility. able to discharge effectually the duties implied in this relationship. The daily cares and anxieties, the constant solicitude, the fears and misgivings and sorrows of the parent, the toils and sacrifices without number, could not be borne but for this implanted and overmastering principle.

Filial Love is the counterpart of parental love, and, while similar to it in some respects, differs from it in others. It

Differs from parental love, how? possesses less strength and permanence. It does not manifest the same steadiness and intensity. There is no such sense of responsibility in the child as in the parent; hence the greater attention prompted by this, and the knowledge of the dependence of the child. These tend to modify the character of the parent's love, and make it different from that of the child.

That this is an implanted principle, and not a cultivated sentiment, is evident from several considerations. It is more abiding than a cultivated affection in most of the relations of life. From persons, not akin to us, to whom we are thus affected, we withdraw our affections, or they subside of themselves, when we find that the objects of them are unworthy. But that a parent has become vicious and unworthy, or even a reprobate in the community, is not ordinarily sufficient to estrange the affections of a child. So, too, while we may feel at liberty to resent certain kinds of treatment by a mere acquaintance, or even a friend, however intimate, it is not so with the child in relation to a parent, — at least, it is not commonly so. Then, too, in these cases, and in some others, when a child comes to treat a parent with disregard, and especially with unkindness, there is a spontaneous feeling of disapprobation, and often of indignation and abhorrence, which does not exist in view of the estrangement of other friends. *An implanted and abiding principle.* *Public sentiment.*

Fraternal Affection, or that felt by children of the same parents, is not so obviously a natural or instinctive sentiment as the affections previously described. Some, indeed, have maintained the opinion that this affection is wholly the result of cultivation, and that it arises solely from the fact that the individuals concerned are thrown constantly together. But this does not account satisfactorily for all the phenomena presented. Others besides brothers and sisters are thrown together for *Some regard it as a result of cultivation.*

long periods. It is true that in such cases warm friendships and close attachments are formed, but these are comparatively few. It is true also, that among brothers and sisters, there are exceptional instances of alienation and unfraternal manifestations. But it will be found that the great majority of those who are not connected by fraternal ties, and are yet thrown into one another's society, do not develop the affectionate regard for each other that exists almost universally among children of the same family.

FRIENDSHIP.

This is a sentiment which exists between persons brought into one another's society, who are congenial and mutually attractive. The reasons for the attachments are very numerous, and sometimes quite unaccountable. The attachment varies from a very moderate regard to an intense devotion. We have some very remarkable instances of these friendships in history, as well as from observation, and that man is poor indeed who is not himself a party to more or less of these happy relationships.

Description of this affection.

GRATITUDE, OR LOVE OF BENEFACTORS.

Gratitude is sometimes reckoned as a simple emotion awakened by a deed of personal kindness. But it is certainly something more than mere gladness or joy, however great, at the acquisition of a desired object. There is obviously an additional feeling, which is of the nature of a particular kind of regard for some person who is the intentional cause of this gratification, and of thankfulness to him. It is a little more

Something more than a good feeling.

difficult to place it among the affections than to distinguish it from the emotions. Still, it is undoubtedly the case that kindness shown to a person does usually awaken affection, sometimes of the most ardent kind. I would not say that this added element of affec- tion is what constitutes gratitude, as distinguished from simple thankfulness, because the affection often exists, and perhaps grows stronger even after the occasion of the gratitude may be forgotten. Still, there is little doubt that some affection is implied in all genuine gratitude.

Kindness awakens affection.

PATRIOTISM, OR LOVE OF COUNTRY.

This is a marked characteristic of most men. An attach- ment partly to the soil on which we were brought up; to the natural features of the region in which we have lived, perhaps from childhood; to the habits and customs of the people; to the government, local and general; to the institutions, laws, usages, and history of the national community, — is apt to beget a deep and fervid feeling, which is peculiar, and which frequently becomes a powerful motive of action. Especially is this the case if the country has been through great trials, and has come out of them successfully and triumphantly, more especially if it is a country under a popu- lar form of government. Then each one real- izes something of a proprietorship in it, and rejoices in its prosperity as in something of his own. Still, I think there is something more and higher than this in patriotism, else we would not have so many brave men enthusiastically following their national flag into obvious perils, and at such great and sometimes ap-

Various ele- ments com- bine to pro- duce this affection.

More con- spicuous under a popu- lar form of government.

palling sacrifices.   There is a kind of national life spring-
ing out of the constituted nature of human
National life.
society, of which every citizen is a partaker, — a
national consciousness and national sensibility, which are
essential elements in patriotism, and to which it owes its
natural and spontaneous character.

THE LOVE FOR HUMANITY, OR PHILANTHROPY.

This affection is unquestionably natural to the constitution of man, notwithstanding the fact that it is often con-
cealed by other interests, as also the fact that opportunities
for its manifestation are less frequent or less prominent
than in the case of most of the other affections.
A positive
affection.
Still, that it is a positive affection, and belongs
to man as man, is evident from a variety of considerations.

Let a man be in any considerable peril, or be swept into
a current and clinging to some frail support, liable to give
way at any moment, if the suspense is protracted
Men in peril.
how deep and universal is the interest excited
in the community!   A large proportion of the population,
perhaps every person able to do so, will hurry to the scene
of danger, and manifest the most intense interest.   This is
not exceptional, but in all ages and nations,
Not excep-
tional nor
both civilized and barbarian, evinces itself in
local.
ten thousand ways.   Let a great fire, or a flood,
or an earthquake, or other devastating calamity, come to a
community, causing wide-spread distress, and making great
numbers homeless, how quickly the benevolent impulse is
felt in remote communities, and among total strangers !

It is indicated, again, by the disposition to build and
endow charitable institutions, such as asylums for orphans,

deaf-mutes, the blind, and other unfortunates ; hospitals for the sick, and dispensaries ; as well as to set on foot enterprises and associations designed to furnish facilities for indigent young people who are seeking education and qualification for useful lives. Benevolent institutions and associations.

It is still further evident in the devotion of good men and women of talent, and sometimes of genius, to the reformation of abuses through which so many are destroyed, and wretchedness is so greatly multiplied. Howard, Wilberforce, Clarkson, Gurney, Elizabeth Fry, Florence Nightingale, Wendell Phillips, and other such persons come instantly to our minds when we speak of such things. Noted philanthropists.

We have the testimony of travellers in all parts of the world, who have found even in barbarous tribes, and among the most uncultured communities, that under the most forbidding circumstances there were always some in whom this feeling of humanity was a living force. Doubtless more of this exists, even in the most degraded communities, than comes to the surface, as it is liable to be repressed by fear or jealousy, or perhaps overborne by some passion or propensity inconsistent with its expression. Even manifest in barbarous tribes.

SYMPATHY.

Sympathy is the feeling that rises on contemplating the pains and sorrows and the unhappiness of others, as also their joys and prosperities. This, also, is by some regarded as a simple emotion, but it seems to me to be so closely related to our love of our fellow-men in more immediate or more remote relations, that it properly holds a place among the affections. Its nature.

It is scarcely possible for a healthy mind, and especially one morally well developed, not to be affected by the emo-

Affected by the emotions of others. tions of others ; and to be so affected is to have similar emotions. That this should be the case is involved in the very constitution of our nature. Even the brutes give indications of these feelings,

Brutes. at least in a rudimentary way. It is not an infrequent occurrence for them to give evidence of being affected by the happiness or misery of their fellow-brutes.

It is more common to use this term with reference to the feeling awakened by the discomforts and adversities of

Awakened by the adversities of others. others, than to those called into activity by their enjoyments and delights. It is true, we do enter personally into the welfare of our fellow-men ; still there is a marked difference, such as I have suggested. There are several reasons for this. One is that sympathy is more useful and more needful in calamity and disaster than in prosperity. For this reason it becomes more emphasized, and doubtless more noticeable. It is also true that joy is more natural than sorrow, and therefore more commonly the heritage of all. For this reason, when the latter comes it is more observable and more exciting.

Sympathy must be distinguished from certain other terms closely affiliated with it. The difference between it and

Not commiseration. **Commiseration** is that the use of the latter is confined to cases of suffering, — it does not express a fellow-feeling of enjoyment or pleasure. **Compassion** was

Not compassion. originally and etymologically the exact Latin equivalent of Sympathy, but in the English use of the two words the meaning has palpably diverged. Compassion, as now used, means the disposition we have towards the unfortunate, when it is in our power to aid them. Sympathy, as we have seen, may exist where there is no possibility of giving any aid. **Pity,** like commiseration, is an emotion excited by the suffering of others, but differs from sympathy in that it is not excited by the happiness of our fellows. It probably differs from commiseration in the fact that the person feeling the pity is usually in a superior position to the object of it. I do not mean by this, as some seem to imply, that there is a feeling of superiority necessarily, much less of contempt, though possibly these two feelings get mixed in the mind sometimes; but that the one who exercises the pity is in a more favored and less painful position than the other.

Not pity.

Difference between pity and commiseration.

CHAPTER VIII.

THE MALEVOLENT OR MALEFICENT AFFECTIONS.

As previously intimated, while Dr. Hopkins's objection to the classification of the Affections as Benevolent or Malevolent has much force, the substitute which he proposes is open to almost equally grave objections. It is for this reason, as well as for the reason that no one is likely to be misled, that I adhere to the old nomenclature.

It has already been shown that the Affections are the most complex of the sensibilities. They differ from the Emotions in having an element of desire; they differ from the Desires and Appetites in the fact that both the latter are self-regarding, while the Affections are altruistic, or regardful of others. This is true of both the Benevolent and the Malevolent Affections. They seek to affect others than the subject. The former aim at some good for others, the latter at some ill. The radical element in the one is love; in the other, hate. It is true that in very many instances neither the one nor the other of these elements is very pronounced; still, in some form, rudimentary or otherwise, it is present.

The Malevolent Affections have many forms. I mention first that of **Anger**. This involves an unpleasant feeling on the part of the subject, which is accompanied by a desire to affect disagreeably the person who is presumed to have caused the unpleasantness.

Have regard to others than ourselves.

Nature of anger.

Anger is the basis of all the so-called Malevolent Affections. Those known by other designations are either modifications of this, or in some way involve it. It is partly instinctive and partly voluntary. The former characteristic applies to those sudden excitations of passion which arise on certain occasions, without thought on the part of the person affected. The latter refers to the feeling that is prolonged, and, perhaps, intensified or otherwise modified by reflection and consideration. Sometimes the feeling excited by some action or other is greatly diminished or wholly nullified when the case is examined, and full account is taken of the circumstances and conditions. On the other hand, an act which at first produces no feeling, or only a slight one, and which is scarcely noticeable, on being revolved in the mind, and considered in certain of its relations, becomes a serious offence, and produces a corresponding increase of unpleasant feeling. Frequently the additional and aggravating elements are from the world of imagination, instead of being found matter of fact, and are fruitful sources of misunderstanding and states of mind for which there is no justification.

Basis of all malevolent affections.

Instinctive and voluntary.

Affected by imagination.

Of instances of purely instinctive anger we have the fact that little children who get hurt by running against some obstacle, are disposed to wreak their petty vengeance on the insensate object. The savage breaks and tramples upon the arrow that wounds him. Even in highly civilized and cultivated persons this feeling is not always absent. I have seen a refined lady, of great prominence in society, take up a pen to write a hurried note, and, finding it good for nothing, dash it from her with great vigor, as if in resentment at its failure to do its duty. For the most part, however, in persons of any considerable discipline and education, this passion is under control. If any fail to govern themselves in this respect, as in many others, a reasonable public sentiment regards it as a sign of weakness and culpability.

Usually regarded as culpable in cultivated persons.

By some it has been denied that this feeling properly belongs to our constitution. It has been thought to impeach the wisdom and righteousness of the Creator to suppose that He should implant in us an element of character which implies hate. He commands all men to love one another, and therefore it would be inconsistent for Him to put a principle the very opposite of this into our nature.

Supposed by some to be inconsistent with our constitution.

But we are to remember, in the first place, that we are now looking at the phenomena of the human soul as they manifest themselves; that is, as they are, not necessarily as they should be. Certainly this is one of these manifestations, and is as nearly universal as any which exposes itself to our observation. If it be a part of our constitution, as it now is, we may reasonably conclude that either the Creator placed it there for some wise purpose, or that our nature has been in some way perverted so that it no longer expresses the design of the Creator.

We are to look at the phenomena of the soul as they are, not as they should be.

Then, again, we see, if we look at the matter carefully, that there are a proper place and use for such a principle; not, probably, in its intense and perverted manifestations, but in its essential and purely natural action. As has been implied, instinctive resentment has no moral character. It acts before reason and judgment have opportunity to furnish any basis for moral

Instinctive resentment no moral character.

conduct, and without their direction. It seems to have been designed to protect persons in case of sudden and unforeseen attacks, where, if time were taken for deliberation and consideration of ways and means, action would be too late.

Voluntary resentment can be justified only so far as it is essential to the welfare of the individual and the protection of society. That a person who in- *Voluntary resentment, how far justifiable.* jures another should be made to pay some sort of a penalty, must be affirmed by the sense of justice in every man's mind. This penalty, before society became developed and organized, must naturally be inflicted by the hand of the individual injured, or, if he were dead or disabled, by the nearest relative. This was the primitive method of the administration of justice, and prevailed far down the history even of organized society. Later came the universal usage among civilized peoples to surrender this individual function to society, which, in turn, undertook to guarantee the protection and defence of the individual. Still, there remains a proper and natural *A proper and natural individual resentment.* resentment towards a person committing a wanton injury. This does not imply that it may not be modified by various other elements of character. A love for all men may easily quench the rising hatred which is involved in anger or resentment. A spirit of forgiveness towards the culprit comes into exercise on the penitence of the latter, often even when this is wanting. A repression of whatever savors of unkindness and vindictiveness will be found in every person of much moral cultivation. But the feeling of resentment is, at the bottom, a natural and not unwholesome element of the human constitution.

MODIFICATIONS OF ANGER.

As has been intimated, resentment or anger is the basis of all the so-called malevolent affections. There are many

Different kinds of resentment. modifications of it, known by different names. **Indignation** is the feeling we have when a palpable and wanton wrong has been done, either to ourselves or to another. **Wrath** is anger intensified, and, as some would say, felt by a superior towards an inferior, though this is somewhat doubtful. **Rage** is a violent outburst of anger, expressing itself in violent language or action. **Fury** is rage venting itself in a still wilder and more extravagant manner. **Revenge,** or **Vindictiveness**, is anger cherished, and seeking satisfaction in some evil done to its object in return for some evil experienced. **Envy** is resentment and ill-feeling experienced when others prove themselves superior to us, and who, as we are apt to think, are less worthy of this success than ourselves. It is usually regarded as a most unworthy disposition, and is universally reprobated. **Jealousy** is akin to envy, and yet is sufficiently distinct from it to have a designation of its own. It is a painful feeling, and one of the most powerful that can affect a person. Its chief peculiarity is, that it is directed towards an object devotedly loved, which, at the same time, becomes an object of suspicion and resentment. The strength and bitterness of the jealousy are usually proportioned to the depth and intensity of the love bestowed. The suspicion or surmise that forms the occasion for the feeling is usually that the person loved is bestowing favor on another, and therefore is withdrawing something from the subject. Under its influence one is incapable of judging correctly of the conduct of the object concerned. Everything is interpreted in the worst possible way, and some of the most innocent incidents are perverted into proofs of guilt.

> " Trifles light as air
> Are, to the jealous, confirmation strong
> As proofs of Holy Writ."

In Shakespeare's drama of " Othello," we have a powerful representation of this passion.

DIVISION THIRD.

THE WILL.

CHAPTER I.

GENERAL CHARACTERISTICS OF THE WILL.

THREE divisions of the phenomena of the Mind have been kept in view from the first. They are the **Intellect**, by which we know, perceive, judge, and reason; Recapitulation. the **Sensibilities**, by which we enjoy and suffer; the **Will**, by which we choose and put forth efforts. It has been clearly shown that these are not divisions of the Soul into *parts*, one of which thinks and knows, another feels and desires, and another chooses and acts. It is the Mind simple and indivisible that is the subject of all these operations. In each individual it is the Ego or Self that does any of them. *I* know, *I* am pleased or pained, *I* choose, — not some part or department of me.

Again, it is to be noted that these different departments of the psychical phenomena are intimately related to each other. They stand in the order of conditioning The different and conditioned. Unless the Intellect furnishes divisions intelligence, or is presumed to do so, there can intimately related. be no feeling; and without the previous affection, and consequent state of the sensibilities, there can be no occasion for choice or volition.

WHAT IS THE WILL?

Let us start with the already implied proposition that the Will is not an *entity*, but a *power*. It is the executive

power of the mind.   It is defined by Dr. Hopkins as "*that*
*constituent of man's being by which he is cap-
able of free action, knowing himself to be thus
capable.*"   Says Dr. Reid, " Every man is conscious of a power to determine, in things which he con-
ceives to depend upon his determination.   To
this power we give the name of *Will.*"   Dr.
Whedon defines Will as "that power of the soul by
which it intentionally originates an act or state of
being;" or, more precisely, " Will is the power of the
soul by which it is the conscious author of an intentional
act."

The Will, though not subject to coercion by any other
power of the mind, or by any power or condition outside
of the mind, nevertheless always acts with reference to these other powers and conditions.   We
can see this better if we take a concrete case.
A poor man comes to me.   I am informed of his wants, and
convinced that he is a proper object of charity.   So far my
intellect alone acts, and my judgment decides as to the
facts of the case.   Further, my feelings are moved.   I sin-
cerely pity the man, and desire his relief.   Here my sensibilities are engaged.   I have at my disposal five dollars,
which I know will supply his need and mitigate his suffer-
ings.   Here intelligence again becomes an element in the
case.   I desire to supply the man's wants with this money,
but I have purposed to myself to purchase with that money
a new book, which promises to be of great utility to me.
I desire to use the money in this way.   Here, again, the
sensibilities are in activity, and with this peculiarity, that
I have two opposing desires, both of which cannot be gratified.   Let us suppose that I will find the greater pleasure

in buying the book. My mind at once inclines to that action, but at this point I become conscious of another feeling — the feeling that I *ought* to relieve this man's want. Here duty opposes itself to inclination.

So far there has been no action of the will, on the main point. I begin to balance the incentives to action implied in the situation. My intellect is working again. It is possible for me to decide either way. I am clearly conscious of this, and there would otherwise be no conflict. There is no power to coerce me. I may decide in favor of my own gratification. If I do this, I am certain, after it is done, that I might have done the opposite. But we will suppose that I decide to do what I ought to do, instead of what will merely please me. I *determine* to give the man the money. This is a real act of the will. The real act I have determined, or, as we say in common of the will. parlance, I have "made up my mind." But the act is not yet complete. There must follow an effort to convey the money to the man. This is what some of our Volition. best writers call *Volition*, as distinguished from *Choice*, or Determination. Others make volition include the choice, and regard the former as the real act of the will. However they are to be named or regarded, here are certainly two distinct elements, or perhaps we may say, two distinct acts. The one follows from, and is consequent upon, the other. It is true the volition Consequent may not follow instantly. I might determine upon choice, yet may not to do a certain deed to-morrow, or next week, follow. but when the time comes the conditions have been so changed as to make it expedient for me to change my determination. It seems to me there is an act of will in the choice or determination made.

As intimated, it would appear that an act of the will is incomplete unless there be, in addition to the choice, a

Choice, as an act of the will, incomplete.

putting forth of effort to carry it into execution. This, where the determination has reference to an immediate action, inevitably follows the decision, but if it be a choice or determination concerning a future action this effort may be postponed, and may never be made It is to be observed here, furthermore, that this effort must be distinguished from the physical action. This is no part of the volition. It is the movement solely in the mind with which we are here concerned.

Dr. Hopkins regards the Will as having these two con-

Two constituents of will.

stituents, *Choice* and *Volition;* and holds that the quality of freedom inheres in the former, and not in the latter.

We find, then, that the act of willing is connected with, and conditioned upon, several other acts of the mind.

Will dependent on other acts.

There is first an intellectual operation. There must be intelligence of objects or acts between which to choose, or there can be no choice. There must also be a desire, or there can be no choice. It is impossible to conceive of a choice among a number of objects in none of which one felt any interest, and for none of which there was any desire. Then there is choice or decision, and finally the effort or volition. This last, we

Volition not physical effort.

are to remember, is not the physical effort; it may stop short of that. It is the effort of the mind to carry out its choice. It usually results in the exertion of physical energy, but the mind, as it moves toward this end, may see, before it comes to the point to affect the physical instrument, that it would be useless.

I may determine to go out of a room, but before I arrive at the door even, I may ascertain that it is so fastened that physical effort would be useless. I therefore abstain from such effort; but, nevertheless, there was a complete act of will, including the volition.

CHAPTER II.

CHOICE AND MOTIVE.

DESIRE, in its relation to the Will, constitutes what is called **Motive**. By some writers this is reckoned as a part
What is mo-
tive? Not a
part nor a
cause of the
willing.
of the willing, and by others it is regarded as the cause of the action of the Will. Most of the recent writers on this subject deny both these doctrines. But motive is so closely connected with the act of the mind in willing, that we need to say a few words about it.

It is unquestionably true that the mind will not act in willing without motives. As has already been seen, it is
Motive an
essential
condition.
impossible to conceive of the mind as making a choice, where there is no desire for any of the objects or acts among which the choice is to be exercised. Hence we may regard the motive as a condi-
A condition
not a cause.
tion of action. But a *condition* is not a *cause*. A cause is that which produces an effect. A condition, though producing nothing, is that without which something could not be. That is, the consequent could not exist without it, but *it* could exist without the consequent.

There may be several **Conflicting Motives** operating upon the mind at the same time. The child desires to eat his
Conflicting
motives.
cake now; he also desires to keep the whole or a part of it till to-morrow. Here are two con-flicting desires operating as motives. Only one of these

can be gratified. They are both reasons why the one or the other action should be performed. But not only do different motives for a choice between two actions or courses of action exist, both of the latter of which may be innocent, but there are classes of motives between which to choose. The most prominent of these classes are motives of pleasure and motives of duty. A young girl desires to go to a party. Her mother is ill, and needs her help. Here is the motive of *duty* conflicting with that of *pleasure.* It is true that desire is an element in both. The girl desires to do her duty, and to help her mother; she also desires to go to the party. It may be that the latter desire is the stronger. She may yield to either. There is nothing that will determine her choice except her own self, but she will be under the influence of both motives, and she may be more powerfully influenced by one than the other. Still, she is compelled by neither. *Alternatives of duty and pleasure.*

There may also come in other motives, subsidiary to those already mentioned. Intelligence may present other facts and circumstances besides those previously observed, and these may operate as influential in the determination of the choice, but the main question will turn on the alternative of self-gratification on the one side, and duty or obligation on the other. *Subsidiary motives.*

In view of all these motives, and under their influence, the choice is made; but it is never so made that it is felt afterward to have been a choice compelled by circumstances, or caused by any extraneous power, or any force outside of the proper personality of the subject. *No choice compelled.*

The word *Choice* needs to be carefully considered, lest it mislead us. It is, by a certain class of writers, regarded as synonymous with *Preference*, and the meaning here evolved easily glides into that of the prevalent desire. But Choice

Choice not preference.

is a stronger and more definite term than Preference. The latter is largely a matter of the Judgment, the former is purely a matter of the Will. Again, the careless use of these words induces the impression that

Determination.

choice is, after all, only the effect of the strongest motive, instead of being entirely free. It would possibly be better if we used the word *Determination* as indicating a purpose formed.

Of the other element in an act of the Will, namely, *Volition*, we have already said what is sufficient for our present purpose.

CHAPTER III.

MAN AS A FREE AGENT.

In claiming the freedom of man, it should be observed at the outset that he is free only within certain limits. We shall best apprehend the limitations if we note the particulars in which man is not free. **Man free only within certain limits.**

In the first place, man's body is not free. This is subject to physical laws, like all other matter, and hence to the necessary operation of physical forces. We can, it is true, to a certain extent control our bodies, but only under the limitation of these laws, and by carefully forestalling their operations. **Not physically free.**

Our intellects are not free, in the sense in which we are now using that word. They are also subject to conditions, and their actions are necessitated by these conditions. We cannot directly choose what we shall know, nor even always upon what subject we shall think, nor at what conclusions we shall arrive. We are *compelled* to know some things, even entirely against our desire and choice. We are necessitated in many of our beliefs. When we open our eyes, or listen with our ears, the sensations produced or the perceptions taken in are not all subject to our will. If we see a horse we cannot will to perceive an elephant, and if we hear the bray of a donkey it will be of no avail for us to attempt to perceive the sound **Intellect not absolutely free.** **Perception subject to its laws.**

of a flute. We cannot will the knowledge of a thing that

Associations. does not exist. So of our associations. They must follow their laws; and, while we can select out of those which present themselves certain thoughts on which we will meditate, we cannot directly determine

Reasoning. which shall present themselves. Our reasoning must follow the laws of thought. In any genuine process of reasoning we are compelled to a particular conclusion, whether it be what we would choose or the very opposite.

Our sensibilities also are under the law of necessity. In

Law of necessity in our sensibilities. certain afflictions we cannot avoid a feeling of sorrow any more than we can suspend ourselves in the air without a support. Nor can we prevent joy and gladness arising in our minds upon their proper occasions.

The Will itself, or the mind in willing, is free only within a certain limited space. As between two contra-

The will free only within a certain space. Must choose. dictory courses of conduct, we *must* choose; we are not free to choose neither. Furthermore, as we have already seen, freedom in willing does not imply freedom in acting. The Will is only the determination to act, the forming of a purpose the

Liberty of choice not liberty of action. execution of which may be prevented by physical or other causes over which the Will has no control. Again, the Will is not free from exposure to influences operating upon it. These are sometimes conflicting, therefore some of them must be resisted in order that the more reasonable or the more desirable may prevail. These influences do not control the mind in its action, but they demand effort and resistance, and hence have in them an element of necessity.

But, small as is the sphere of the soul's freedom, such a sphere exists, and within it the soul is free in the most absolute sense conceivable. Its freedom cannot be invalidated. No power nor thing can act there save the mind of the subject. Even God himself — let it be reverently said — shuts himself out from any interference with it, by the very constitution he has given to man. Within this sphere man is sole master of himself and of his eternal destiny. Here he forms his character, whatever that may be, and by this product he must be judged, and from the judgment there is no appeal. *[Freedom absolute within its sphere.]*

The reasons for this opinion have been given, or implied in part. There are others, which we may consider while alluding to those previously mentioned. First, we must appeal to the *conscious experience* of every person capable of understanding himself. This is the tribunal to which we must bring a certain *[Testimony of consciousness.]* very large class of questions for decision, principally those pertaining to the operations of the mind. The *Inner-Sense*, or, as it is popularly called, *Consciousness*, is the only means we have of knowing anything about these operations. I do not say that some persons, under peculiar conditions, may not take certain opinions for the deliverances of the Inner-Sense which are not so. But if this organ of cognition fails us, we have no other, and if we cannot trust its decision we can trust nothing. For, even our perceptions, for the most part, depend upon what we know to be the state of our mind in sensation. Still, whatever might be the error of exceptional individuals, concerning the testimony of the Inner-Sense in isolated instances, the agreement of the great mass of intelligent men generally, and upon any one particular subject, ought to settle it beyond reasonable doubt.

Now, it is unquestionably true that the great mass of men, in all ages and nations, and under all conditions, have believed themselves to act freely. They never for a moment doubt this when following their spontaneous and natural convictions. In innumerable instances, after an action, they are sure that they might have done differently from what they actually did. If it be a matter of obligation, they condemn or approve of their conduct as it would not be possible to do if their action had been caused by forces or personalities outside of themselves. No one thinks of blaming himself for being in a certain place if other persons have taken him by force and carried him there, nor does a man accuse himself of crime if another person has forcibly put the hand of the former upon the trigger of the pistol, the firing of which caused the death of some one.

Universal belief in individual freedom.

Closely connected with this is the approval or disapproval which we feel in view of the conduct of our fellow-men. No one is disposed to condemn a man for an act of which he does not think him guilty, and he certainly does not regard a person guilty of an act which he could not help doing, or which he was actually compelled by other forces or conditions to do. The very conception of responsibility involves that of freedom, and to hold one responsible for an act concerning a deed in relation to which he had no real freedom of action, would be cruelly unjust.

Approval and disapproval of the acts of others.

Responsibility implies freedom.

It is here that our judgments of men's conduct are somewhat modified by the character and circumstances of the actor. The great mass of the influences operating upon him, and inclining his mind in one direction rather than another, affect our own decis-

Our judgments modified by circumstances.

ions in the consideration of the case. We do not blame a child for the same act to the same extent that we blame a man. A semi-idiotic person receives lighter condemnation than the substantially sane man, while one totally idiotic is not judged at all. It follows, then, that there are different degrees of approval; which further implies that the power of the Will varies at different times and in different persons, and that the forces influencing the Will are greater or less at different times. It is conceivable that these forces may be so strong as to overcome the power of the Will. In that case there is virtually no will, no freedom, and no responsibility, and hence no judgment concerning the subject, any more than in the case of a brute or of a tree. *If influences are controlling, then there is no will.*

Another modification comes in here. The weakness of a mind in willing diminishes the severity of our condemnation only when this weakness comes from no fault of the person concerned. If it is the result of a series of evil choices, by which he has demoralized himself, and then been rendered incompetent, we still hold him responsible, and condemn his evil choices, as well as all their results. So, on the other hand, when a man, by habitually willing the proper things, has come to a condition in which his will is easily superior, and dominates his whole personality, holding in subordination his lower powers, and then having liberty in its largest and most genuine sense, we give him credit for this, as well as for particular acts which are right. *Weakness of will may be caused by the subject.* *So of strength of will.*

CHAPTER IV.

THE WILL NOT A SUSCEPTIBILITY, BUT A POWER.

IT has already been stated that the Will is *not an Entity*, but a *Power*. It is to be remarked here, that, being a power, it is *not a Susceptibility*. Those who hold that the action of the Will is determined by motives make it the latter instead of the former. Yet it seems to me that every person must be conscious that the Will is a positive power, and not a mere passive instrument. If it were true that the mind, in willing, is controlled by the strength of the motives operating upon it, it would follow, as Dr. Schuyler has shown, that in at least a considerable proportion of cases the action would not be in the direction in which either of the motives acts, but it would be a resultant of the two. Thus if, out in the public square, I hear two men at different points calling me, if I have an equal desire to go to each of them, a combination of the impelling motives will carry me, not in the direction of one of them, but in a diagonal to some point half way between them. Suppose the motives are not equal; still I should not be carried to either point to which I wish to go, but to some other point, nearer that of the stronger attraction. Only in the case where one of the motives was *nil*, should I be impelled to go directly to one of the points. This is a very mechanical illustration, but then the doctrine that the strongest motive causes the

(margin: Not a susceptibility.)

(margin: Effect of the composition of forces.)

action of the mind in willing is a purely mechanical doctrine, — an attempt to apply a physical law to spiritual
things. It is a matter of the power of motive, as determining the action of the mind in willing. I see no other
way but that of two or more motives, each of which must
be supposed to have some force which cannot be annihilated
by that of the other. There are cases where the impulsions
are in entirely opposite directions. In such cases the
stronger motive will impel toward one object and away
from the other, but whether it would ever cause the subject
to reach the former is more than doubtful. This on the
hypothesis that motives cause action.

A motive, then, is never a cause of the mind's action in
willing, but rather a reason why the mind thus acts, — a
condition of its action in a particular way. There *Motive the*
are those who deny that a motive is necessary, *reason why, and not the*
even as a condition ; but this absence of motive *cause.*
appears only in the case of two contradictory desires so
exactly balancing each other as to practically
annihilate the force of both. It is doubtful if, *When mo-*
tives exactly
in such a hypothetical case, the mind ever puts *balance each*
other, the
forth the power of choice ; and, even if it does, *force of both*
annihilated.
the instances are so extremely rare that they are
of no practical consequence, and even speculatively are
hardly worthy of consideration.

The difference between a *cause* and a *condition* has already
been pointed out. The fact appears evident that the power
of the Will is an uncaused cause, or a **First Cause,** *The will a*
not to the extent and in the infinite degree that *first cause.*
God is a First Cause, but just as really as He is. It is a
supernatural power, the only element in man's constitution that makes him superior to nature, and able to sub-

ordinate it to his uses. Without it he becomes a part of nature, subject to its laws and forces, and compelled to

A finite first cause just as real as an infinite first cause.

drift on in its current, whithersoever that may move. As an animal, man is subject to these laws and forces. The appetites and passions dominate him. The strongest has right of way, and he must yield to it, as do the other animals. But as *man* he is conscious of a power in him which makes him superior to nature, and enables him to control the forces which control other animals and all other objects. When appetite

Man the master of his cravings.

craves gratification, he is not only competent to determine whether that gratification is wholesome and right, but also to refuse it indulgence. So of other cravings, as also of the passions. The fact that men sometimes do not assert their superiority only adds emphasis to the doctrine that they possess it, inasmuch as they feel a sense of degradation when they have failed in its assertion, and submitted to these lower forces. Other men, too, contemn such surrender; and both the sense of self-degradation and the contempt of others arise from the fact that all men recognize the existence of this power superior to nature, and that it is the part of every individual man to assert it.

CHAPTER V.

MORAL CHOICE.

It has been implied all along that the mind, as a preliminary to choice, in many instances deliberates, considers the facts and circumstances, the concomitants and Preliminary consequences, of an act or its alternatives, the deliberation. pleasures and pains of which it will be the antecedent, and that there is frequently a struggle in the mind Sometimes a before a decision is reached and the Will acts. struggle. I say, this is true in many instances; probably it is not so in all. Perhaps in a great majority of cases the decision is made as soon as the occasion is presented. Often the de- Those instances in which there is a struggle are cision imme- usually those in which the choice lies between diate and without de- pleasure or self-interest on the one side, and liberation. duty on the other. There may be deliberation in other cases, and doubt as to what is most advisable, and sometimes conflict of opposing interests, but these are more easily decided than the conflict between interest and duty. There is also a marked difference in the consequences of such decisions in the self-judgment of the subject. In the conflict between the different kinds of self-interest, the main question is, in which the real interest lies; and when this is settled the Will for the most part accepts that decision, and by its own act ratifies it at once. But it is not so always in the struggle between duty and self-interest. Sometimes it is long protracted. The mind inclines now to the former, now to the latter. In the former case the

decision is referred to as wise or unwise, prudent or imprudent; it produces satisfaction or regret, as the case may be; but there is no remorse necessarily. In the other case there is approval and self-complacency, or disapproval and condemnation, — a sense of guilt and degradation.

It is not intended to insist here that this distinction between the different classes of motives, or between desires

and obligations, is always clear and obvious. There is a tinge of obligation frequently in the most self-regarding desires; as, for instance, a man may hesitate as to whether he shall use a certain sum of money in his possession on a pleasure excursion, or shall with it purchase an additional piece of ground or some additional machinery, either of which will be of advantage to his business. Here, at first sight, it would appear that there is nothing in the question save the gratification of one of two desires, either of which is legitimate. But it may be that the question has a certain moral character also. Possibly the condition of the man's health demands the rest and recreation. There may be danger of his breaking down by continued application to the absorbing cares of his business. Duty to his family, as involved in the preservation of his health, may come in as an element. Or, on the other hand, if the contemplated excursion is one of mere pleasure, with no ulterior object, and the investment of the money in his business is something very important, and, it may be, essential, and to spend the money for anything less important will be something like waste, — here the element of obligation would be present again, but in the other scale. Or it may easily be that both these alternatives have a strong moral coloring, from the fact that, on the one side, health is imperilled, and it seems a duty to take care of that, and, on the other side, his business may suffer, and duty also requires him to guard that. So that what at first appeared a mere matter of preference between two self-regarding desires becomes a conflict of possible duties.

But in general the distinction is clear enough for practical purposes, and we may say that whenever there is an important conflict of motives it is usually between duty and inclination, or obligation and the desire for pleasure.

This brings us again to the office of the Will in the construction of character. It will probably be denied by no one whose opinion is of much account, that *Office of the will in the construction of character.* desired and striven for by every man. It will *of character.* also be readily admitted that the order of precedence in the principles that are to govern man in the construction of his character is, first *the right*, then *self-interest*, and then *appetite* and *passion*. It does not require any long argument to show that to give appetite and pas- *Appetite and passion rank lowest.* to man's greatest happiness on the whole, nor to the securing of the noblest and the perfect character. Nor need we spend much time in showing that *Self-interest subordinate to right.* would not produce this coveted effect. The assertion by every man of his individual interest as the foremost principle of his action would operate to the detriment of society, and, consequently, to the harm of all its members, since society is valuable to its members only in proportion as it approximates perfection.

But if the universe and humanity are wisely constituted,

the great law of right must be paramount, and in obedience
Law of right to it the interest of individuals must be more
paramount. fully promoted than by any other possible ar-
rangements, and the happiness of each will, in the long
run, be greater than by any other policy.

It is here that we see how Will, as *a governing purpose,*
is an interesting feature of our constitution, as well as of
Will as a great importance. It is thus that it exercises
governing its power as a creator of character. At some
purpose. time in the early history of every individual the
question arises, Shall I make my own enjoyment, immediate or remote, the predominating principle of my life, or
shall the doing of right be the paramount purpose? This
may be settled by the formation of a general purpose to
lead a strictly virtuous life, or it may take the purely
religious form of always doing, at whatever sacrifice, all
that God desires us to do. There may be a long struggle,
indecision, vacillation, before this purpose is formed. It
may be broken after it is formed, but in multitudes of
cases it becomes the settled principle of action. This now
The final and is the final and supreme end of this man's action.
supreme end He has willed this, and all subsequent volitions
of action. are to be subsidiary to this. The Will becomes
a fixed state of mind, — a perpetuated will, so to speak.
Worthiness of moral character, the real worth of the soul,
has come uppermost, and not undermost, in the plan of life,
and he calls upon every impulse, and desire, and purpose,
to adjust itself to this.

He may, on the other hand, determine to make individual
happiness or interest his chief good, excluding his own
The opposite worthiness, or making it subordinate, and bend-
interest. ing all his energies towards this end, and thus

radically depraving himself, and rendering his disposition altogether bad. This prevailing purpose may not be in the mind all the time. Attention may be directed at times wholly to the subsidiary volitions and purposes, but the other is the constant aim.

CHAPTER VI.

COMPLETE INDIVIDUAL LIBERTY.

LIBERTY is sometimes distinguished from freedom, but the difference is not great enough to be of any value for our present purposes, and may as well be ignored. I wish, however, to speak of liberty in a slightly differ-

Liberty in a modified sense.

ent sense from that in which it has been hitherto used in relation to the Will, and yet having reference to substantially the same general signification. The inquiry which I now propose has to do with the perfect liberty of the individual,— in what it consists, and how attainable.

It has already been remarked, that if a child were to attempt to explain its conception of liberty, it would very

The child's definition of liberty.

likely say, *It is having everything we want, and nothing that we do not want.* This is very common and idiomatic language, but it is probably about as correct an expression of the real idea as could be conveyed in more philosophical terms.

Now it is evident that no person with whom we ever come in contact possesses this large, full liberty. Every one

No one in possession of this perfect liberty.

has something which he does not want, and which he would a good deal rather not have; no one has all he wants. It is furthermore evident, that, with most of us, our wants and desires oppose and restrict

Our desires restrict one another.

one another. They are in such conflict that the gratification of one implies a denial of another. Something always must be sacrificed in order that something else may be enjoyed. In other words, our nature is not harmonious, and it is only in the harmonious operation of our powers and susceptibilities that perfect liberty is found.

Is this perfect liberty attainable? It may be rash to predicate even a possible perfection of man in his present state; but certainly perfect liberty for the indi- Is perfect vidual is conceivable, and towards the realization liberty attainable? of this conception every one is moving who has formed that *governing purpose* of which mention was made a few pages back. We all know some men and women who have made much progress in this direction. The simple fact is, the grand ethical object of every man who has set his proper end before him is to attain a perfect character, and a perfect character implies perfect liberty. It is not difficult to understand that men are, in We are under this world, under a system of law. By their a system of law. Our own conduct in part, and in part by hereditary mal-adjust- influences, they are in mal-adjustment to this ment to it. system. It presses unequally upon them, it produces discord, the desires of the soul run counter to each other, they oppose and conflict with each other, while in the ideal or perfect character they would be parallel, and thus harmonious. The object of all ethical training is to remedy this evil condition of confused and conflicting interests, — to get the character adjusted to the laws. Whether any do perfectly attain to this in the present life, is not a question for discussion here; but this we know, that many even here make great advancement in this direction. Many go far In proportion as they approximate it, they are in this direc- tion. free in the only sense possible to any intelligent being in the universe. In other words, complete adjustment to the moral law will subordinate every desire to this one purpose, and will bring all the before discordant desires into perfect harmony; and this is the perfect liberty which the soul craves.

This is a state in which one does what one wants to do, and does nothing else, and has what one wants to have, and has nothing else, simply because he wants only what the Divine law requires, and he has that. His desires now

*Desires par-
allel with
God's desires
parallel with
each other.*

run parallel with this law, and hence are parallel with each other. Conflict is impossible. This will help us to understand the wonderful meaning of the expression, "**Liberty under Law.**" No other liberty is possible to beings constituted as we are. It is not by getting rid of the restraints of law that men are made free, but by adjusting themselves to law.

This will help us to understand another thought which has sometimes wrought a little confusion. We believe

*Liberty of
glorified
saints.*

that there are beings in the universe who have arrived at a state in which we regard it absolutely certain they will never do what is wrong. All who believe in a future life have no doubt that some, at least, of those who have lived here in the world will attain to this state. We frequently speak of this state as one in which those attaining to it *can* do no wrong. This, I take it, is not true nor consistent. If they *cannot* do wrong they are compelled to be virtuous, and this is not liberty; it even seems to me to be not virtue. I see no reason why the loftiest and purest spirit in the universe *cannot* do wrong. It is certain that he *never will*, and that because he infinitely *does not want to.* He has become perfectly adjusted to the great law of the universe, and he has no desires running counter to it. Hence there is no motive to violate it, no reason why he should do so, and men do not act without motives or reasons.

This may be illustrated by a very simple analogy. For the most part, no man ever puts his hand into the fire. This is not because he cannot do so, but because he does not want to. The analogy is not quite perfect, but nearly enough so for our purpose. It is possible that there may be a sufficient reason for a man to put his hand into the fire. It is not possible that, to a soul such as we are supposing, there should be any reason for violating moral law.

> We do not put our hands in the fire, not because we cannot, but because we do not want to.

CHAPTER VII.

NECESSARY IDEAS PRODUCED BY THE COMBINED ACTION OF THE INTELLECT, SENSIBILITIES, AND WILL.

As we saw in studying the Intellect by itself, there are certain necessary cognitions which are given us by the very energy of the Mind. So there were seen to be certain other cognitions which necessarily arose, which are the product of the Mind, as Intellect and Sensibilities combined. We are now to find that there are still other similar cognitions, which the Mind, as combined Intellect, Sensibilities, and Will, furnishes by its own power. I follow here the course so admirably marked out by Dr. Hopkins in his "Outline Study of Man."

Reference to necessary ideas previously considered.

PERSONALITY.

The first of these cognitions which we shall consider is *Personality*. As Being connects itself with all the cognitions of the mind as Intellect, and as Good underlies and is implied in all those products for which we are indebted to the combined Intellect and Sensibilities, so Personality is present in, and gives character to, all those ideas to which the combination of the Intellect and the Sensibilities with the Will give rise. All the characteristics of the mental products of which we are now to take note are *personal* characteristics, and pertain to man simply as he is a person.

Personality closely related to all the other necessary ideas.

Personality cannot be defined. It is simple, and there-fore cannot be analyzed. It may be bounded off from other cognitions, but generally each one must go to his own consciousness for an account of it, and we can do little more than direct attention to it, with this end in view.

Undefinable.

A *Person*, then, is distinguished from a *Thing*. Person-ality belongs to a being having intelligence. self-direction, responsibility, freedom of moral action, and con-sciousness. It belongs to a being knowing him-self as the originator of certain movements from within himself, who also knows himself at one point of time as identical with himself at some other point, and that he is the same, self-persistent and inalienable from his substance.

Person and thing.

POWER OR CAUSE.

I put these two notions together, not as being identical, but as being intimately connected, — so intimately, that it is hardly possible to think of one without a suggestion of the other. Cause, I think, always implies *Power*. It is not so certain that Power always implies Cause. It seems to me that we may conceive of Power as existing while not operating as Cause, — quiescent, inac-tive power, power as capability.

Cause implies power.

Dr. Hickok asserts, and with some reason, that Power is not phenomenon, but notion. It is clearly not a matter of perception. But I do not think, as he seems to think, that it is a product of the Discursive Fac-ulties. It is rather a product of the Reason, or the Regula-tive Faculty. We know it as we do other cognitions of this class, on the occasions on which it presents itself as Cause. The knowledge of it springs up on every such occasion from

Power not phenomenon.

the very energy of our minds; we cognize it because we cannot help doing so. It is a necessary idea.

Probably our first cognition of it is always in our own personal exercise of it. We will a movement, we put forth a volition, we realize that we are furnishing the beginning of a series of operations. We are powers, and we know ourselves to be such as certainly as we know anything whatever.

Its first cognition in our personal exercise of it.

A certain class of philosophers deny that causation implies power. They claim that it is simply another name for *Invariable Antecedency.* If one event always precedes another, they set it down, according to a general formula, that the former is the cause of the latter, and that there is no other condition but that of antecedent and consequent. But this fails to commend itself to the common-sense of man. Whether the average man can form any tolerable conception of cause or not, he is quite apt to make a clear distinction between it and a mere *antecedent.* No one ever thinks of regarding day as the cause of night, or night the cause of day, though they follow each other in invariable succession. In a country where buzzards and other birds of prey abound, a dead carcass will be the invariable antecedent of their gathering where it lies, but no one thinks that it compels them to gather. As Dr. Hickok says, we may imagine two sets of wheels of two each. In one set the two are driven by separate powers, and yet so arranged that the cogs of the one wheel invariably match those of the other, each following each in perpetual succession. In the other set the construction is such that, one wheel being moved, its cogs drive the other. There is invariable succession in each case. But any person of ordinary intelli-

"Invariable antecedency."

Dr. Hickok's illustration.

gence will see at once that in the former case one wheel is *not* the cause of motion of the other, while he will see that in the latter case one *is* the cause of the other's motion. There are many instances in which one event follows another where both are caused by a common force, but it would be nonsense to say that, because one invariably follows the other, the latter is the cause of the former.

It has been maintained by some authorities that the idea of cause has been gained from experience, or observation of habitual repetition. That this is not so, is evident from observing the knowledge of cause in very young children. If you roll a ball along the floor and knock down some toy ten-pins, the two-year-old child, without having witnessed any such phenomenon before, knows that the rolling of the ball is the cause of the falling of the ten-pins, just as well as if he had seen it a thousand times. He wants you to do it again, sure that the same consequent will follow. That is, he is certain that the same cause, under the same conditions, will always produce the same effect. If you build up a house with little blocks, and then, with a dash of your hand, knock it down, making a racket, the child can hardly wait till you build it up again before he imitates the stroke of the hand, knowing very well it will produce the same effect. "A burnt child dreads the fire," and it usually does not require more than one burn to make the dread effectual. He is more certain of the effect than he ever can be made by a hundred parental cautions and instructions.

Not gained by experience.

The young child knows it as well as an adult.

It seems clear enough, then, that a *Cause* is an antecedent that has *power* to compel a consequent, and that our notion of Cause originates in our own consciousness of power to produce effects. this con-

An antecedent with power.

sciousness being occasioned by some putting forth of power
The axiom implied. by our own will. The axiom connected with it
is, as Dr. Hopkins says, " Whatever begins to be
must have a cause."

FREEDOM.

The doctrine on this subject has already been substantially set forth. The origin of the idea of Freedom remains
Origin of the idea. to be only briefly considered. It is a product of
the combined action of the Intellect, the Sensi-
bilities, and the Will. It is a *necessary* idea, and, like all
necessary ideas, it comes from the inherent energy of the
mind whenever the occasion for it is presented. The occasion in this case is that of the exercise of the
The occasion. power of choice. " Let the opportunity or the
necessity of choice between two different kinds of good be
presented, and the idea of freedom at once emerges. Let,
for instance, a man be required to choose between property
and integrity, and he knows by necessity, and with a conviction which nothing can strengthen and which nothing
can shake, that he is free to choose either. The discussions
about the freedom of the Will have been endless, but nothing has ever shaken the conviction of the race in regard to
the elementary idea of freedom as involved in choice." [1]

RIGHTS AND OBLIGATION.

These are correlative, and consequently suggestive each
of the other. When an individual has rights, every other
Correlative and mutually suggestive. individual is under obligation to respect those
rights. Rights are closely connected with means
of happiness or *good*. When a person has himself produced what is a means of good to him, there arises

[1] Dr. Hopkins: Outline Study of Man.

spontaneously in his mind, and in the mind of every other person cognizant of the facts, a conviction that he has a right to that product and the use of it. Here *Origin of the* the idea of right emerges. It is an original and *idea of right.* necessary idea. Also, some other beings may be so related to us that we are responsible for their good, and they are dependent on us for direction and control. Here again the idea of right arises, as also the idea of obligation.

Dr. Hopkins traces the conception of obligation to the opportunity of choice between a higher and a lower good, and insists that here is where this idea first *The idea of* arises. It would be impossible, he thinks, for *obligation.* two such objects of choice to be presented to the mind, and not be accompanied by the obligation to choose the higher. Here, too, as he teaches, is where the notion of moral right [1] emerges. He endeavors to show that an act is not right in itself, except as it implies the choice of a higher good than that involved in the alternative. This may or may not be true. I have no disposition to discuss the question here. But certainly we somehow, in the contemplation of actions or objects among which to choose, feel that to choose one of them is right, and to choose the other is not right, and we instantly are aware of the obligation to accept the right and reject the wrong. Here we come upon the idea of obligation, and we come upon it, as I think, nowhere else.

Obligation, then, is from the Intellect and from the Sensibilities; it also has relation to the Will. "As *Obligation* from the Intellect it is rational; as from the Sen- *related to in-* sibility it is emotive. It has in it, therefore, an *sibilities, and* element both of reason and of impulse, and so *will.*

---

[1] It is necessary to distinguish between *right* as the quality of an action, and *right* as pertaining to the individual.

is capable of becoming, and does become, an authoritative impulse. But an authoritative impulse is law, and, so far **An inward law.** as we can see, is the only possible form in which there can so be a law within the constitution, that a man can be a law unto himself. As authoritative, law must be both promissory and minatory; for anything claiming to be a law without a sanction, expressed or implied, would be no law. But if promissory and minatory, then of what? It must be of some good on the one hand, or of evil on the other, that may be realized in the sensibility." [1]

But we must apprehend the real nature of obligation. It is impulsive, not compulsive. We often use the term **Obligation not compulsory.** *obliged* as if merely synonymous with *necessitated.* It is not so. A child is obliged — that is, under obligation — to obey his parents, as all men are also to obey God. This means merely that he *ought* to do so, but he is not necessitated or compelled to do so. It is possible to violate an obligation, and men often do this. It is true, as we have seen, that such a violation has its necessary penalty, as the fulfilment of the obligation has reward. These, however, operate as motives, and motives, as we have seen, are influential, but not compulsory.

MERIT AND DEMERIT.

These are also original and necessary ideas, occurring to the mind only on certain occasions, and sure to arise then. Obligation furnishes the occasion, or, rather, the fulfilment **Their nature.** or violation, of an obligation. There is not only a feeling of discomfort and degradation when

---

[1] Dr. Hopkins.

we have violated an obligation, but there is an expectation of consequence, a sense that there is connected with the act some ill desert. In both these, there is an intellectual element, an idea; and it is this idea that always arises by the mind's own energy on the occasion of fulfilling or violating an obligation, and in no other way.

RESPONSIBILITY.

We have already made some allusion to Responsibility, in discussing the subject of Freedom. Like the other terms which we have just considered, it indicates both a feeling and an idea. It thus has an element from the Intellect and an element from the Sensibility. It is also dependent on the Will, or rather upon the freedom of the mind in willing. For, as has been shown, no such thing as responsibility is thinkable unless the mind acts freely, and is the originator of its own choice or volition. The idea arises when the occasion of choice between two objects or actions presents itself, and a moral obligation is implied to choose one of them rather than the other. I *ought* to do this, says Conscience. I desire to do that, but *ought not*. The obligation does not constitute the responsibility, but it implies it. The obligation may be to one person, the responsibility to another; or rather, perhaps I should say, there is both obligation and responsibility to another. As, for instance, a parent sends a child to return a toy which he has borrowed from a playmate; he is under obligation to the playmate, but responsible to the parent.

Dependent on the will, as free.

Responsibility unthinkable without freedom.

Responsibility differs from obligation.

PUNISHMENT.

This idea originates on the occasion of violated obligation, and is a necessary idea. We must discriminate between that which is the mere consequence of an action, and the punishment for a violation of obligation. If by mistake I drink a cup of poison, which I thought to be prescribed medicine, and am made sick, this is a consequence. Perhaps we may call it a penalty of a violated natural law, but not a punishment. But if I steal, and am arrested, tried, and convicted, and sent to prison, the imprisonment is, it is true, a consequence of my act, but it is something more, — it is a punishment. The idea is different and peculiar. It is found nowhere else but on the occasion of an act freely committed, but in violation of an obligation, and for which the person committing it is, therefore, responsible, and to which, in my mind, the notion of demerit necessarily attaches itself. There is the expectation of a consequence that is not merely natural and unpleasant, but which is distinctly punitive.

Differs from consequence of action.

Penalty and punishment.

It will be readily seen that all the foregoing ideas are impossible, except on the supposition that the subject is free in his willing, and thus has the power to give character to his own acts.